D1713939

Lil Mama From The

Projects 2

By Mz. Toni

Acknowledgements

This Book Is Dedicated To Janaya Shanice Lynch My Baby Sister Gone Way Too Soon......

I am so blessed and humbled by the amount of love I've received for this series, to those readers who stuck with me since IIWYW series I appreciate you to the fullest, and to my new readers thank you for giving me a chance!!! I want to thank my test readers Tarina Wright and Shana O'gilvie, I also want to thank my awesome publisher Tiece Mickens for believing in my craft and allowing me to drive her crazy, My Miss Mickens/Tiece Presents Family for all their help and love. Kellz Kimberly, Yas and Briana for pushing me with these word count challenges, and to the editor who did the damn thing.

Facebook: Author MzToni

Instagram: Toni60962

Chapter One (Cherish)

"I love you too," he replied. Kissing me on my lips, he held me and rubbed my stomach until we both fell asleep. A loud noise woke me from my sleep, and when I opened my eyes, I was staring down the barrel of a gun. It was dark so I couldn't make out whose face it was.

"Bitch, you thought this was over. You killed my fucking dad!" Meeka screamed.

"I thought you were dead?"

"Tell ya fucking friend to get her aim game right!" she said laughing. Looking over, Mega was gurgling and choking on his own blood.

"Mega noooooo!" I screamed, rushing to his side, he was shot in the stomach and blood was everywhere. I was trying to apply pressure to it with a sheet, like I'd seen done on TV, but it wasn't working.

"You thought you would live happily ever after bitch!" she laughed before pulling the trigger.

Waking up in a cold sweat, I literally felt like I was having a heart attack, my chest was tight and I couldn't breathe. Tapping Mega, he jumped up with his gun waving until he noticed that it was just me and there was something seriously wrong.

"What's wrong lil mama, is it the babies?" he asked with a worried expression.

"I can't breathe, something is wrong!" I said frantically.

"You gotta slow ya breathing down!"

"I feel like I'm gonna die!"

"You're not gonna die, you're having a panic attack, one of my foster moms used to have them all the time, control ya breathing," he said, rubbing my back.

"I can't Jason!" I snapped. I felt like I would die at any moment and this nigga wasn't calling 911, he was rubbing my damn back.

"Come here," he said, pulling me in between his legs. As he rubbed my stomach, he asked me questions that I felt were irrelevant.

"What you think we having?" he asked.

"I don't know Jason damn!"

"Alright, well we gonna have two bad ass boys," he said with a smirk.

"No, I want a girl, so we gonna have a boy and a girl," I replied.

"What we gon name them? I like Mega," he said.

"No, ya mama ain't name you Mega, our son's name will be Jason Cruz Jr.!" I snapped. Before I knew it, we were having a full conversation about the babies and my breathing was normal.

"Oh my God it went away!" I said surprised.

"I told you it was just a panic attack; it feels worse than it is."

"Thank you," I replied, kissing him.

"You good lil mama. That bitch dead and never coming back and I need you to believe that."

"But how do you know?" I asked. I could feel my breathing quickening again and my hands were getting sweaty.

"Yo chill out before you hurt my sons. I wouldn't tell you something that I didn't know Cherish," he said while holding me.

"Ok," I reluctantly said before dozing back off in his arms.

The next morning I was tired as hell, I got no sleep last night. Things with me and Mega have been great, I didn't get a chance to make it to my graduation, but I did get my diploma in the mail, which was good enough for me. Mega has been on his best behavior and has been waiting on me hand and foot. I don't know how women do pregnancy because this shit was horrible to me. I was always sleeping, even when I slept all day long, I would usually sleep all night long. I was always eating weird shit, like yesterday, I had Mega drive to the mall to get me some

Cinnabons and when he brought it, he had a look of disgust on his face when I added a bunch of sour cream. I don't know what it is about that shit together but it tastes so good, but then I'll be farting the shit out for days. The only good thing is that I don't get morning sickness. I heard when the man gets the sickness that means the baby will come out looking just like him. Today was my four month check-up and even though I know they say I gotta wait a month, I just hope these babies spread them legs so we can see what I'm having. Between me, Mega and Camille, these babies have more than enough to last them a lifetime.

"You ready for your doctor's appointment?" he asked while I was getting ready.

"Hell yeah I'm ready!" I said laughing. After we were both dressed, we headed out to my doctor's appointment. I knew Jasmine's bad ass was gonna be upset because she tried to talk us into letting her stay home so she could go to this appointment. Walking outside to the car, Mega helped me into his truck and we headed out. When we got to the doctor's appointment and were called back, the nurse wasted no time flirting with my man like she always did.

"Hey Mr. Cruz, you're looking good today." she said with a smile.

"What's up?" he responded back.

"Uhhhh don't you need to be doing something, I would hate for you to be fired for not doing ya job," I said to her while she stared at Mega with lust filled eyes.

"Oh yeah my bad," she said before taking my blood pressure and temperature.

"Your pressure is a little high, the doctor will talk to you about that when he comes in," she said before walking out.

"That bitch lucky I'm pregnant!" I snapped at Mega when she walked out.

"Stop being so mean lil mama," he said laughing.

"I ain't being mean, that bitch is straight disrespectful!"

"Cut it out, that's why ya pressure high now, you stressing about nothing," he said, shaking his head.

"Oh trust me, I ain't stressing over that bitch!"

"Yo Camille really pulled you out of ya shell," he said licking my ear.

"Stop it Mega damn," I said with a smile and slight moan.

"Let me taste you."

"You are nasty; I ain't fucking you in my doctor's office," I said pushing him away. Since being pregnant, we been fucking like rabbits and I ain't even complaining. I never knew I could want sex as much as I did these last couple of months. Sometimes I would get to the point where I wanted to cry because he was too busy to give me some.

"Come on lil mama," he said, rubbing my kitty through my pants. Before I knew it, he had my pants undone and pulled down and he was working my kitty with his fingers. As soon as I was about to cum, the doctor walked in. Mega went to move his hand, but my horny ass locked my legs tightly so he couldn't, the doctor quickly closed the door and I came hard as hell.

"You calling me nasty but it's ya horny ass that's nasty!" he said with a smirk before sticking his fingers in his mouth to taste my juices. While I was fixing my pants, the doctor knocked on the door.

"Come in," I said shyly.

"Hello Ms. Daniels, hello Mr. Cruz," he said with a smirk.

"What's up doc, my bad about what you walked in on."

"It's no problem, but to prevent this from happening, I would advise you guys to get a few off prior to the appointment,"

he said, causing me to blush from embarrassment, but Mega started laughing like the doctor told the funniest joke.

"I tried to tell her to stop but you know how these pregnant chicks be," Mega said, lying through his fucking teeth.

Punching him in his arm, I gave him the look of death. The doctor performed my ultrasound vaginally and we still couldn't tell what we were having, I was pissed.

"Oh these babies are being stubborn," the doctor said with a laugh.

"Yeah like their mama," Mega replied. After me and the babies were checked and told everything was good, I got a date for my next visit and we headed out. When we got inside the car, the ride was silent as we listened to the radio. While he was driving, my ringing phone interrupted our thoughts.

"Hello?" I asked after answering the phone for a number I didn't have programmed.

"Hi sweetie, this is Ms. Lisa, Shameeka's mom," she said in a sad voice. Motioning with my hand for Mega to turn the radio off, I put Ms. Lisa on speakerphone.

"Oh, hi Ms. Lisa," I replied.

"I have some really bad news and I wanted to call you first seeing as y'all were best friends."

"Well you know, me and Meeka had kind of grown apart, but is everything ok?"

"They found her body in some abandoned house downtown in Camden," she said before sobbing loudly.

"I'm so sorry to hear that Ms. Lisa, you have my deepest condolences," I said shaking my head. Was I sorry that

Camille killed her ass? Hell no, but I did feel bad that it had to come to that.

"It's ok baby, she was staying out all night, doing that damn coke and wet, she had really let herself go when you two fell out," she said sadly. I wanted to tell her the truth; that her lying sneaky ass daughter always did drugs and hung out with the wrong people, but I kept it to myself because she deserved to remember her daughter the way she wanted to.

"If there's anything you need, just let me know."

"I would love it if you could say a few words at the funeral, nobody knew Shameeka better than you, and I'm sure she would've wanted that." As soon as those words left her mouth, I could feel my heart quicken and become tight.

"Oh no Ms Lisa, I can't do that," I said hyperventilating. I watched as Mega pulled the car over, I don't know why I kept getting these damn panic attacks, but they were scary as hell. Grabbing the phone from me, Mega talked to Meeka's mom.

"Hey Ms. Lisa, this is Cherish's boyfriend, she isn't feeling too well so I will have her call you back later," he said before hanging up.

"Lil mama calm down, you gotta slow ya breathing down."

"I can't talk at her funeral, I hate that bitch!" I said through tears.

"You don't have to," he said, rubbing my back.

"Talk to me like you did before, help me think of something else," I said holding my stomach.

"I'm thinking about hiring some help," he said while rubbing my back.

"Help where, cuz I ain't with that nanny shit, ain't nobody gonna be watching my babies but me," I snapped.

"Calm down, I'm talking about help at the office," he said laughing.

"Oh, well if that's what you want to do, I'm sure you would be less busy," I said feeling my breathing slow down.

"Yeah, that's what I was thinking. Especially when the babies come, I wanna be there to help."

"Oh and you will be so go ahead and hire you a little secretary," I replied with a laugh.

"Yo, you bossy as hell now a days," he said.

"Whatever and you better not hire no big booty ho either," I said jokingly.

"You feel better?" he asked, kissing my forehead. Nodding my head yes, he started the car again and pulled off. When we got home, we waited for Jasmine to be dropped off by the school bus. When she came home, I fixed dinner while Mega helped her with her homework. A few days later, Meeka's mom called me again about talking at the funeral and I had no choice but to lie to her. I knew if I didn't give her an answer she would continue to call, so instead, I said fuck it and came up with the best lie I could.

"Hey Cherish, I'm not sure if you know, but Meeka's funeral is in a few days and you never called me back to say whether you would speak or not."

"I can't do it, I'm pregnant with twins and I really can't handle the stress of the funeral."

"Oh I didn't know you were pregnant, you were never really the boy type," she said laughing.

"Yeah, I guess it just took the right boy."

"How does your mother feel about it?"

"Me and my mom don't talk anymore, you know how strained we

"Yeah, I used to tell Meeka all the time when she used to say she hated me that she could have been given a mother like yours."

"Yeah, I would have taken you as a mom any day."

"That's so nice of you to say, I just wish my own daughter felt that way about me."

"I'm sure she loved you, she just never got around to saying it."

"Cherish, I loved Meeka, she was my child, but she wasn't a very good person, God rest her soul she wasn't. I guess that's why I really wanted you to speak at her service because I don't have too many nice things to say about my own child and that breaks my heart," she said before sobbing.

"Meeka had her ways about her, you're right about that, I mean you're her mom and even you have to dig deep to find something genuinely nice to say about her. I know you loved her, but Meeka wasn't an easy person to love, so don't fault yourself for how she behaved."

"I can't help but think, maybe if I would have showed her more love, or maybe got her some help when I saw her slipping, she might still be here."

"You can't keep thinking about what you should've done, you'll drive yourself crazy like that."

"You're right, thank you for talking to me, please don't be a stranger now that she's gone and congratulations again," she said before hanging up.

Chapter Two (Mega)

Shit with me and Cherish been good as hell. Sometimes she can overreact, but Camille said that's just her hormones, so I try to deal with it. Today I was meeting with a few candidates to fill the position as my secretary. I told Cherish about my idea and she said she didn't want no big booty ho's, but what the fuck, I run a record label, niggas wanna see a bad bitch, myself included. When the first chick walked in, she was bad as hell; she was definitely someone I would hire.

"Please have a seat."

"Thank you," she said with a smile.

"So, do you have your resume?" I asked.

"Resume, naw I don't have one of those," she said with a confused look.

"Ok, so why should I hire you?" I asked.

"Because I'm the next Beyoncé; I can sing, dance and I can act," she said before standing up and singing. It was bad enough that she was trying to audition at a fucking interview that was solely for a secretary, but the chick sounded horrible. I felt like I was sitting at the judge's table for American Idol and that ain't do shit but piss me off.

"Ok stop!" I screamed, only to have her start dancing around my office. I was about to call security if she ain't sit her ass down somewhere.

"So do I got the job?" she asked out of breath and tired as hell. She had sweat pouring down her face and I think the heel on her shoe broke.

"Naw you ain't got the job!" I said shaking my head.

"Why not?" she asked, placing her hands on her wide hips.

"Because I need a secretary, not a singer."

"But this a record label ain't it!" she had the nerve to ask with an attitude.

"Yes, but I clearly explained the job description," I said becoming annoyed.

"Well I can type and shit too," she said before sticking some gum in her mouth.

"Naw, you can go."

"Whatever!" she said before grabbing her purse and limping out. The next few women that I interviewed were the same exact way, ratchet and looking for a come up. I was about to just cancel the rest, until a beautiful, professionally dressed woman walked into my office.

"Hi, I'm Jayda Rae," she said extending her hand for me to shake. She had a whole stripper name. These bitches killed me changing their names to shit that's nowhere near what they mama done named them.

"Nice meeting you, I'm Jason Cruz, please have a seat."

"Thank you," she said with a beautiful smile.

"Do you have a resume?"

"Yes I do, and before you ask, I want to work at your company because I know I will be a major asset to you. I am determined and I work hard, not to mention I don't have any kids, or a husband, so I will be at your beck and call when needed."

"Wow, your resume is good, most of your jobs were in Atlanta, are you new here?" I asked.

"Yes, I'm originally from Atlanta but I needed a change, so here I am."

"Well, when can you start?"

"I can start tomorrow!" she said excitedly.

"Oh ok, I figured you needed time, but if you don't that's cool."

"So, I'm hired?"

"Yes, the pay is $25.75 an hour, plus gas mileage."

"Wow, thank you so much," she said jumping up and shaking my hand.

"No problem. I just signed a ton of new artist, and I hate to toss you to the wolves, but we will be pretty busy so for the next few weeks, consider this your home. If you can't handle it, let me know, if you can then the human resource office is down the hall and I will see you tomorrow."

"I can handle anything," she said sexily with a wink, before walking down the hall to human resources. God damn her ass was fat as hell, her ass was so fat it looked paid for. That was the kind of ass niggas like me lived to see. Well the old me, the new me had a beautiful daughter, a gorgeous wife and twins on the way that I didn't want to risk losing so I was gonna keep my dick in my pants. As I fantasized about digging all up in Ms. Ray's guts, my phone rang and I knew by the ringtone who it was and instantly felt bad about thinking about another woman.

"Hey lil mama, everything good?" I said after I answered.

"Yeah, these damn babies got me sleeping all day, but can you bring me home some chicken and coleslaw from KFC."

"I got you big mama," I said jokingly, only to have her bust out crying over the phone.

"Why would you call me that Jason?"

"I was just playing."

"Have I gotten that big?" she asked. As we were talking, Jayda walked back into my office looking good. Giving her the signal to hold on a minute, I continued to talk to Cherish.

"No, you haven't gotten that big. I'm sorry, it was a joke and I shouldn't have said it."

"Really, you didn't mean it?"

"No, now stop crying."

"Ok, I love you."

"Love you too," I said before hanging up.

"Was that your wife?" Jayda asked.

"Yeah, she's pregnant with twins so every second she crying," he said with a laugh.

"Oh wow, pregnant? Congrats," she said with a smile.

"Thanks, so did Helen take care of you?"

"Yeah she did, so I guess I'll see you tomorrow," she said licking her lips.

"I guess so," I replied. I don't know if this family life was starting to bore me or what, but I knew that I was a little too hyped to see Jayda. Naw I ain't doing shit wrong, ain't like I'm gonna fuck the chick, what's the harm in a little flirting. When I finished up at work, I headed home after stopping and getting Cherish her food. When I got home, they were both sleeping and dinner was on the stove. If there was one thing I could say about Cherish, it's that she always made sure we were taken care of.

Chapter Three (Cherish)

"Hey babe, I'm leaving," Mega said kissing my forehead.

"Damn already? Ok, well love you."

"Love you too."

"Did you ever find a secretary?" I asked before he left.

"Yeah, she's nice and she works hard," he said nonchalantly.

"Oh ok, why didn't you tell me?"

"I don't know, I guess it slipped my mind. I've been busy as fuck."

"Oh ok, well at least you like her."

"Yeah, she does her job and goes home."

"Is she married?"

"Naw, I think she got some cats though."

"That's that old lady shit," I said laughing.

"Yeah, but let me get out of here," he said before leaving.

Getting me and Jasmine dressed and ready, we headed to go have a lunch date with Camille and her children. Jasmine had gotten really close with Mylee and Sparkle, and I'm glad because they made her adjust with the shit that went down with her mom easier. When we arrived at the Cheesecake Factory, like usual Camille was late. As we sat waiting for Camille, I pulled out my phone to call Mega. Things have been a little weird around the house because he isn't really there anymore. I know his label has taken off quickly, and I'm happy for him, but what about his pregnant woman and his child that he has at home. I don't mind taking care of Jasmine and I love her like she's my own, shit I feel like she is my child, but we should be doing this together.

"Hey boo, sorry I'm late," Camille said hugging me.

"It's cool, hey girls," I said speaking to the kids.

"Hey Aunt Cherish, you look pretty," Sparkle said kissing my cheek.

"I feel like a whale, but thank you baby," I said with a laugh. After ordering, me and Camille caught up.

"So, what's up?" she asked.

"I got a phone call the other day, from Meeka's mom."

"What that bitch want?" Camille said.

"Ooooo mom!" Mylee said laughing.

"I'm sorry baby, but what she call you for?" Camille asked.

"They found Meeka and she wants me to talk at the funeral."

"Man you ain't got to do that shit, all that girl put you through."

"Yeah, I just don't want it to look weird that the person she was with everyday for years didn't even show up at her funeral."

"You ain't got to fake the funk, you did nothing wrong, so drop this shit. Anyways, how are you and Mega?"

"Girl, he working on his label and artist so he's barely home," I said sadly.

"Did he hire the secretary?"

"Yeah, he did."

"Did you meet the bitch?"

"No, but the way he described her she's an old lady or some shit," I said laughing.

"Oh ok well, why not bring the romance to the office?"

"Ooooo yeah, you can pick out something cute," Sparkle's little ass said jumping into our conversation.

"Uh huh you better mind ya business, matter of fact, go take Jasmine to wash her hands so we can go," Camille snapped.

"Ok..." she said pouting. After she left, we continued our conversation.

"What I was saying is that if he is working, why not surprise him, take him some food, have a lunch date with ya hardworking man."

"But it's Saturday and I have Jasmine."

"I'll take Jasmine and keep her overnight."

"Aight, then imma order him something from here and take it to him," I said with a smile. After I ordered his food, we talked for a little while longer and headed out. When I pulled up to his office, I was excited to see my baby. When I walked into his office, he was talking on the phone. While he continued to talk, I moved some of his paper work off his desk and placed his food in front of him.

"Thanks babe," he said, kissing me after he hung up the phone.

"You're welcome. I miss you and you're always here," I said sadly.

"I know. I'm tryna get this shit popping for us."

"I know."

"Hey, Jason, do you need anything before I go to lunch?" someone said from behind us. When I turned around, I was beyond taken aback.

"Uh… naw, thanks Jayda," he replied nervously.

"Who are you?" I asked walking over to her.

"I'm Jayda, his new secretary, and you must be Cherish," she said with a smile.

"Yeah, I'm Cherish," I said shaking her hand before looking at Mega with anger and confusion.

"Well, it's nice to meet you. I've been spending everyday with your man and I must say you're lucky," she said with a smile. When she said that, I instantly didn't trust her. That shit raised my antennas completely and I wasn't feeling her.

"Is that right?"

"You can go now Jayda, have a good lunch."

"Well, we usually go to lunch together, but I see you have yours so see you in a little bit," she said before walking out his office.

"I should slap ya sneaky ass!" I snapped.

"You ain't gon slap shit, you better calm down before you get my babies hyped," he said with a smile.

"Mega I ain't playing with you, why you lie!"

"I ain't lie about shit."

"You ain't say shit either. You made her seem like some ugly old ho!" I screamed.

"How you gonna be mad at me because you assumed some shit!" he snapped.

"Whatever, you knew I would have a problem with this shit, which is why you ain't say nothing," I said. I wasn't no hater, and I wasn't usually the jealous type, but this girl was bad as hell. She looked to be about 5'9 and she was stacked with DD breast and a big old ghetto booty that you can't tell me she ain't pay for. Not to mention, her face was flawless, hair flawless, makeup flawless, while I'm standing here all swollen with my farting ass.

"I don't want her lil mama, I got who I want."

"That doesn't stop her from wanting you. Don't act like you ain't hear the bitch throwing shade."

"She didn't even say shit. I been working a lot and we have been grabbing lunch together," he said with a confused face.

"Whatever, just don't keep shit from me Mega."

"My bad, I should've told you what she looked like."

"Seriously, because that shit makes you look sneaky and I don't like it."

"So you want me to fire her?" he asked.

"Does she do a good job here, or did you hire her for her looks?"

"Come on now, stop tryna play me. She really is a go worker."

"Well, keep her if that's what you want, I trust you," I said, meaning it. I trusted him, but I damn sure didn't trust that bitch and I would be popping up more often now that I knew what the bitch looked like. When I got home, I couldn't stop thinking about this chick Jayda and the shit she said. Mega didn't see it, I guess because he wasn't a female, but I saw the shit, that bitch wasn't fooling me. See, people think because I'm young that I'm dumb as well. She wanna be throwing subliminals and of course, Mega didn't see it cuz he can't see shit beyond how fat her ass is. Ain't nothing wrong with hiring a little eye candy, something you can look at while you work. I ain't one of those jealous chicks that fly off the handle for no reason, but when I see some shit I don't like, that's when the problems come. She can try me if she want cuz she picked the right one and I don't play when it comes to mine.

Chapter Four (Jayda)

ѡould've thought that a simple Indeed job posting
. me to find the man that I wouldn't mind spending
th. of my life with. Things have been so hard for me these past few months, and this is nothing but fate working its beautiful hands. When I walked into his office for my interview, I knew I had to have him. Finding out his little girlfriend was pregnant, I ain't gonna lie was a little setback, but everybody knows a little set back makes for a big comeback. I have been spending everyday with him because of work, but little does he know, I've been getting to know him as well and falling deeper and deeper in love. Ain't nothing like a nigga with swag out here getting shit, and that's Jason Cruz. He is an entrepreneur and I know a good thing when I see it, not to mention he fine as hell. When I saw his little girlfriend, yeah she cute or whatever, but she got that pre-teen body. A nigga like Jason needs a grown woman and that was me. She all insecure and shit, yeah I saw how she was looking me up and down and I heard them arguing when they thought I left. Why would they be arguing and fighting if I wasn't having an effect on his ass.

"Hey Jason, how was your lunch?" I asked when I walked into his office.

"It was cool, my bad about my girl, she pregnant and tripping right now," he said shaking his head.

"You good, how old is she anyway?" I asked, already knowing the answer.

"She's seventeen; her birthday is in a couple months."

"Oh, you like em young huh?" I asked with a smirk.

"Naw I love my girl, but I never dealt with anyone her age before."

"Oh ok. She cute, I saw she was a little upset."

"Yeah, she was surprised to see you. I kind of downplayed ya looks and shit," he said looking everywhere but at me.

"What you mean?" I said taking a seat in front of him.

"Man you know you bad as hell. I ain't want her to get mad so I basically said you was hit."

"You told your girlfriend I was ugly Jason?" I asked before laughing.

"I didn't say ugly, she just assumed you were."

"So you think I'm bad Jason?" I asked licking my lips.

"Look at ya face, look at ya body, come on now, you know you bad," he said with a smirk.

"Well thank you," I said before crossing my legs. I watched him look at my thighs as if he wanted to fuck me right on the desk.

"Yo, you trouble," he said laughing.

"What you mean?" I said standing up and walking in front of him.

"I mean exactly what I said," he replied before adjusting his dick in his pants.

"You seem like a man who likes trouble," I said bending over. My face was directly in front of his, I just knew what was gonna happen next.

"You can go home, we done here," he said before getting up and walking away. That shit pissed me the fuck off. I stood shocked for a few seconds before picking my jaw off the ground. After finishing up some last minute things at the office, I headed home where my roommate and best friend were waiting for me. Pulling up to our apartment, I was still mad about Jason's ass not taking all this sexy bait. When I walked into my apartment, some dude was fucking my best friend Ashley. I would join in and get fucked real good, I was into girls and guys so I didn't mind fucking her, and she was bad as hell.

"What the fuck is going on?" I asked while standing at her door butt naked.

"Hey boo, I didn't even hear you come in," she said while getting fucked doggy style. See what I liked about Ashley was that she was a big ass hoe, an even bigger hoe than I was and she wasn't ashamed of it. I met Ashley while in Atlanta, we both worked at a gentlemen's club and we instantly clicked.

When I told her I was moving to Jersey, she said that's where she was originally from and wasted no time packing her shit and coming with me.

"Who the fuck is that, she bad as hell!" the dude said hyped.

"Shut the fuck up, who told you to stop fucking me!" Ashley snapped.

"Can I join?" I asked sexily.

"Come on boo, he can't eat this pussy right anyways so I need you," Ashley said with a smile. We fucked four hours straight and all my tension and anger was relieved after all that fucking. After we were done and satisfied, we kicked his ass to the curb. He cursed us out while grabbing his shit, but I ain't give a fuck as long as he got up out of here.

"Y'all bitches are crazy!"

"Yeah whatever nigga!" I said before lighting a blunt. When he left, me and Ashley continued to fuck until we tapped out. Dozing off, I woke up to my phone going off like crazy. Looking at the time it was three a.m. Jumping up, I grabbed my phone and quickly answered it.

"Were you sleep?" Jason asked.

"It doesn't matter I'm up now, what do you need?" I replied.

"King didn't get his contract, he's at the club and we need that like now," Jason said frustrated.

"Ok ok, I'm getting up right now, send me the address," I said tiredly. After getting dressed, I was on my way out the door when Ashley stopped me.

"Where you going?"

"Gotta work," I said shortly.

"You doing this for that nigga Jason?"

"Yeah, but I get paid to do this."

"Why not just say fuck him? We have fun together; you know how I feel about you."

"I already told you, I like pussy, but dick is my thing," I said with a smirk before walking out the door. When I got to the club, it was packed. Walking in looking like a bag of money, all eyes were on me. Scoping out the club, I headed towards the V.I.P section with my briefcase in hand.

"Can I speak to you King!" I screamed over the loud music. He looked at me and motioned for the bouncer to let me through.

"What's up sexy?"

"I work for Jason Cruz and Epic Records; I brought your contract here," I said taking a seat.

"Damn and here I thought you were here for me," he said with a pout.

"Business first, pleasure later," I said with a wink. After he signed the contract, some chicks walked up trying to get his attention and that was my way out. Yeah he was fine as fuck, but he was too close to home, wasn't no way I would get Jason if he found out I was fucking the artist. Grabbing my phone, I called Jason to find out where to drop his contract off at.

"Yo," he answered sexily.

"Hey, I got it signed, sealed and delivered," I said with a laugh.

"Bet, you a life saver Jay," he said making me smile. Here he was giving me nicknames and shit.

"Where can I bring it?"

"I'm at home right now, but you can bring it to me," he said before telling me his home address. When I pulled up, I was shocked his house was mini mansion status. I really wanted to go in and see what my future home would look like, but he was already waiting for me outside. Hopping out the car, I turned around to get my briefcase out of the back seat. When I bent over, I could feel his eyes on my huge ass.

"Here you go," I said handing him the contract.

"Hmmmp, where you go looking like that?" he asked.

"You sent me to a club, I had to fit in, you don't like it?" I asked spinning around.

"Hell yeah I like it," he said with a laugh.

"I like what I see too," I said looking down at his dick print through his silk pajama pants. Like most niggas unknowingly do at the mention of their beefstick, he grabbed it and repositioned it. Damn this nigga was working with a monster, and soon it would all be mine.

"You funny," he said.

"I ain't being funny, just real," I said with a wink before switching back to my car, leaving him stuck. When I got inside my car, I rolled the window down, blew him a kiss and burnt rubber out of there.

"Yeah, he was definitely feeling ya girl," I thought to myself as I drove.

Chapter Five (Cherish)

Waking up out my sleep, from yet another bad dream, I looked over at the clock, it was four a.m. and Mega's ass wasn't in the bed. Jumping out of the bed, I called his name only to be ignored. Looking out the window, I saw him and that bitch Jayda. I was confused as to why she would be at my house at four a.m. Watching them interact, my blood boiled. I could see by how she was moving that she was flirting and I could see by the way Mega was smiling that he was loving that shit. When she pulled up, I went and sat at the edge of our bed and waited for him to come upstairs.

"Where were you?"

"I went to get something to drink," he said, giving me lie number one.

"You sure that's what you were doing?" I asked.

"Yeah, what the fuck, why you acting funny?" he asked as I looked him up and down, ready to slap his lying ass.

"Because ya dick is hard as a rock and I saw that bitch outside my house!" I snapped before slapping him.

"Cherish, keep ya fucking hands to ya self!"

"Why you lie?" I asked.

"I knew you would react like this, she was bringing me a contract!"

"So why ya dick hard?" I asked.

"Man my dick always hard!" he said. I knew he was lying because he was way too hyped.

"Yeah whatever, you keep telling me I don't have shit to worry about, but every time I turn around ya ass is lying!" I said grabbing my pillows, getting ready to walk out the room.

"Where you going?" he asked grabbing my waist.

"I'm sleeping in the guest room. I don't want to be around you with a hard dick that some other bitch gave you!" I said before slapping him in the head with one of my pillows.

"Lil mama, you really acting crazy."

"Shut up, just quit fucking talking to me, you big dummy!" I said shaking my head and walking out. Going into the guest room did nothing but piss me off even more because I couldn't sleep without his lying ass beside me. He was really making me feel some type of way. Like if you don't like her and she don't like you, why you gotta lie about shit pertaining to this bitch. With a lot on my mind and my self-esteem in jeopardy, I vowed to myself that before I let this nigga turn me into the weak little bitch I used to be, I would leave his ass and never look back. The next morning, I woke up bright and early to get Jasmine up and ready. I was still pissed about what happened last night, but I would never slack on my duties with Jas.

"Good morning," Jasmine said when she came into the kitchen while I was finishing up breakfast.

"Good morning baby, how'd you sleep?"

"I slept good, what you making?" she asked.

"Some pancakes and sausages."

"Yayyy my favorite!" she said causing me to smile. After making our plates, we sat down and started eating. I was surprised as hell when Mega walked into the kitchen. He hadn't really been around to eat breakfast with us, so I assumed he had left already.

"Where's my pancakes?" he asked with a smile.

"Ain't no more!" I snapped.

"Ooooo daddy you in the dog house," Jasmine said laughing.

"Come on Jasmine, you gotta catch ya bus. Go get ya book bag," I said.

"Why you being like that?" he asked.

"Mega, stop talking to me," I said while cleaning up the kitchen.

"Damn, I'm sorry!" he snapped. Pulling me to him, he kissed my neck while rubbing my stomach.

"Listen, I'm telling you right now, I'm not gonna be one of those chicks sitting in the house pregnant while you out doing you. What we have right here is different, and I understand that."

"What you mean different?"

"You helped me, you saved me and I'm thankful for that, but come on, I saw the girls leaving your house before we met. I know how you use to get down and that shit don't leave easily just because you started messing with me."

"I love you lil mama, and I wouldn't do anything to hurt you."

"If I find out something is going on between you two, I'm done. Please don't make me look stupid Jason," I said honestly. Grabbing me tight, he kissed me passionately before placing light kisses all over my face.

"My bad lil mama for making you feel like this, you trust me?"

"Yeah I do, but I don't trust that bitch."

"Well trust me when I say I don't want her."

"She's a cool ass chick and I want for y'all to get to know each other."

"I knew you were fucking crazy. Please tell me why I would ever be friends with that bitch."

"You being petty as hell. That girl just moved here, she don't know no fucking body and the lil mama I know would at least try."

"That goes to show I ain't the same young and dumb chick. That ho tryna get my man and I ain't with it!" I said not budging.

"You are something else," he said kissing my lips and grabbing a handful of my ass.

"That's why you love me, right?"

"One of the reasons, but how did you sleep?"

"I keep having these dreams and I don't know what to do," I said with teary eyes.

"Maybe you should talk to someone; you suffered a lot of abuse lil mama."

"Maybe you're right. I will look into it today."

"I'm ready!" Jasmine screamed. Walking away from Mega, I went to walk her to the bus stop. After the bus picked her up, me and Mega talked a little more before we both headed out. I was throwing a little get together at Mark's club for Camille and him, and even though he owned it, and knew a party was happening there Friday, he had no clue that it was for him and Camille. While shopping, all I could think about was Mega and how he asked me to befriend a bitch that I knew for a fact wanted to fuck him. Then gonna try and flip shit talking bout the lil mama he know, it's obvious I ain't the same person and I never want to be that person again. I can honestly say me becoming friends with Camille was one of the best things that happened to me. After ordering the cake and meeting up with the party planner, I was ready to go home. These damn babies were taking a toll on my ass.

Chapter Six (Mega)

Damn my lil mama wasn't playing no games when it came to Jayda, she refused to even give her a chance. I knew if she just got to know her she would realize that she was cool as shit. Jayda was like a female version of me, she was confident, bold, smart and straight to the muthafucking point. Maybe she was crushing on a nigga, and yeah we flirted every chance we got, but she knew what it was, it was all harmless.

"Good morning boss man," Jayda said with a smile as I stepped into my office.

"What up Jay, thanks again for helping a nigga out."

"No problem, that's my job."

"Yo, my girl been acting real funny since finding out that I hired you."

"Funny how?"

"Jealous, angry, insecure."

"Well she is pregnant, so that might be what it is."

"I don't know, but I wanted to invite you to my close friends surprise engagement party. Cherish and all of our friends will be there, so I figure this is your chance to break the ice."

"I don't work for her; I work for you Jason, so what if she don't like me."

"Yo, happy wife equals happy life. She's pregnant and I'm not tryna stress her out anymore than she is, so if she was to really say you had to go, I would have no choice but to let you go."

"Oh I see who runs shit," she replied with a smirk. I guess she thought that she was pushing my buttons or testing my manhood.

"Yeah, aight," I said walking into my office.

"My bad for catching an attitude, I'm just so used to females not liking me for no reason."

"It's cool," I said going over some paperwork.

"Are you gonna text me the address?"

"Yeah I got you, it's this weekend," I said grabbing a piece of paper and writing down the address. While writing it down, my stomach growled loud as hell. I was so use to waking up to a home cooked meal every morning.

"Damn, you hungry?" she said with a laugh.

"Hell yeah, I'm starving."

"Wifey ain't feed you?" she teased.

"Naw, I'm in the dog house."

"Awwwww poor baby, I'll order you something," she said before getting up and switching her thick ass out of my office.

Today was another busy day for me, so time flew by super fast and before I knew it, here it was almost nine p.m. and I still wasn't home. I had to make sure all my artist were satisfied, I needed to get the permits for my video shoots, so much had to be done in so little time.

"So you like it out here?" I asked Jayda, taking a break from working.

"It's ok, but ain't nothing like Atl," she boasted.

"Yeah, it's cool, but I wouldn't live there, it's nice to visit though."

"That's because you don't like traveling or change," she said surprising me.

"How the fuck you know that?" I asked confused.

"I can tell," she replied nonchalantly.

"Damn, seems like you know me more than my girl."

"Maybe I do," she said getting up and standing in front of me. Placing my hands on her hips, I felt how soft and nice her thighs were. As she stared at me with lust-filled eyes, I couldn't help but look at the picture on my desk of Cherish and Jasmine at the Cape May Zoo. Taking my hands off Jayda, I walked away. When I got to the bathroom, I tossed water on my face.

"Yo, I need you to chill the fuck out, we love Cherish!" I said to my dick. I walked out of the bathroom and back into my office, only to find Jayda naked on my desk.

"Put ya clothes on Jay."

"What you mean, I thought you wanted this," she said confused.

"You know I got a girl."

"So you don't want me?" she asked sexily.

"Naw, I'm going home," I said shaking my head. Grabbing my shit, I left out of there with pussy on my mind. When I got home, I hopped in the shower, and when I hopped out, I was ready to give Cherish the business.

"Lil mama, wake up," I said kissing her naked back. Licking her lower back, I started to go lower until she let one loose right in my fucking face.

"Hmmmm mmmm," she moaned in her sleep with her stinking ass. I ain't even want none no more after that shit. Lying down beside her, I kissed her neck and took my ass to sleep.

Chapter Seven (Cherish)

Tonight was the night of Camille and Mark's engagement/wedding party and I was too excited. The party planner I hired took care of everything from the food down to the decorations, so all I needed to do was come out of my pockets, which for me as of lately wasn't a big deal.

"Hey lil mama, you ready for tonight?"

"Yeah, I'm ready, are you?" I asked Mega.

"Why you say it like that?"

"You been coming home later and later Mega."

"I've been busy."

"You sure about that?" I asked.

"Man don't start that shit. I can't even get none because you never feel like it anymore, a nigga ain't used to this shit!" he snapped, hurting my feelings.

"You got some fucking nerve. I am almost six months pregnant with fucking twins and you talking to me about how you can't get none. Shit I'm bloated and swollen and fucking tired after taking care of Jasmine and this house!"

"Man I don't even eat here. Jay brings me lunch and dinner," he said.

"Oh yeah, does she, well how about you be with that bitch and leave me alone. I'm so tired of hearing about this bitch!"

"I'm out, I'll see you tonight!" he said before leaving. I can't believe that nigga had the nerve to say some shit like that to me. That bitch Jayda got him feeling himself and he gonna make me bring him down three fucking notches. Grabbing my phone, I called Camille with Shana on the line also. While I waited for them to answer, I pulled out what I was wearing tonight.

"Hey boo!" Shana said happily.

"Hey Shana. Camille, you on the phone?"

"Yeah, I'm here. Hey y'all."

"Well, I got a problem. Mega is being super disrespectful because of this new big booty hoe he hired."

"Wait, I thought you said she was old!" Camille screamed.

"That's what I thought until I showed up to his office and in walked a fucking video vixen."

"Why didn't you tell me?" Camille asked.

"I don't know, I wanted to give him the benefit of the doubt and I knew you would fly off the handle."

"You damn straight. You pregnant and he with this bitch most of the day because she works closely with him," Camille said. I didn't even have to explain because Camille knew the whole run down already.

"Exactly!"

"So now she probably telling him what he needs to hear right now, looking all sexy and now the grass starting to look greener," Camille said.

"Oh my God, you think he cheating!" I said breaking down.

"Bitch, you such a debbie downer. You don't know if Mega cheating with that bitch, and I don't think you should make any big decisions until you know for sure," Shana said.

"Just do what you feel," Camille said.

"I just don't want him to get use to disrespecting me as if it's cool," I said.

"You gotta put ya foot down. You can't be weak when it comes to our niggas because they will take advantage in a heartbeat!"

"Y'all still going to Mark's club tonight, right?" I asked them.

"Hell yeah we going!" they said. Shana knew the party was for Mark and Camille, but Camille just thought it was a regular party for someone else.

"It sucks that ya pregnant ass can't come and turn up!" Camille said hyped.

"Girl, I never really went out anyways so it ain't like I know what I'm missing," I said laughing.

"Your birthday is in a few months; maybe you should live a little once you hit eighteen," Shana said.

"Imma have two newborn babies Camille, my fun is over before it even starts."

"That's where women fuck up at, your life ain't over, you have friends like us willing to help and you have money bitch, get you a nanny. I love Mama Betty but I had to get someone permanent and I ain't worried about her around my man cuz Ms. Mary bout old as hell and she good with the kids."

"I don't wanna push my kids on someone else; I can take care of my babies myself," I said seriously.

"Alright boo, I'm just tryna help," Camille said.

"Well, I gotta start getting dressed," Shana said.

"Ok, I'll talk to y'all later," I said before hanging up. After hanging up with my girls, I thought I would feel better, but I didn't. I wasn't in the business of keeping a nigga that didn't want to be kept, so if the shit he said to me was really how he felt, that's a huge fucking problem for me. Tonight was the party and tomorrow was my first appointment with a therapist I found online. Getting up, I went to get ready for tonight. I was wearing black jeggings, a dressy maternity shirt and some wedge sneakers. I still looked good, and most importantly, I was comfortable as hell. Once I was dressed, it was already eight and the party started at nine, which meant I needed to hurry up, drop Jasmine off at Mama Betty and get to Mark's club. Grabbing Jasmine, we headed out. After dropping her off and talking to Mama Betty for a little while, I headed to the club. It was packed and the bad part is that the shit was closed out to the public until midnight, so everybody here was here solely for Camille and Mark.

"Hey John," I said hugging the bouncer.

"What's up Cherish, how you doing baby?"

"I'm good, how you and the wife?" I asked with a smile.

"She working a nigga nerves like usual."

"Give her a break, you niggas are hard to handle," I said laughing

"Yeah, aight. I fuck a bitch every now and again, she knew how I was when she started fucking with me," he said with a smirk that rubbed me the wrong way.

"Well, I will talk to you later," I said shaking my head and walking into the club. When I got to the V.I.P section, Kasan, Chris, Mega, Shana, Queesha and a bunch of people I had never met before were chilling.

"Hey Cherish, you did this shit girl!" Queesha said hugging me. The entire club was decorated in silver, black and white, it was really beautiful. While talking to the girls, I watched as Mega stared at me with his puppy dog eyes, I could care less. I had to deal with people bringing me down and hurting my feelings because I didn't have a choice, but I refused to be with a nigga who thought he could talk to me the way Mega did earlier. Walking over to the buffet table I had set up, I piled my plate with some good ass soul food and sat down to eat while dancing in my seat to the music. I expected for Mark and Camille to be late but God damn, not this late. Walking outside, I pulled out my phone and called to see where they were.

"Hey boo, where you at?" I asked when she answered.

"Girl, Mark's ass done pissed me off, but we on our way to the club, why you ask?"

"Just was wondering," I said with a smile. After hanging up, I walked back into the club. A half an hour later, Mark and Camille were walking in.

"Oh my God!" she screamed when we surprised her.

"You did this?" she asked looking at Mark.

"Naw, I'm as surprised as you are," he said shaking his head.

"You did, didn't you?" she said looking at me. Running over, she gave me a big hug while thanking me over and over. I knew she might be emotional because as much as she loves me, I know she wishes that her actual best friend was doing this.

"I love you boo," I said kissing her cheek. After being all emotional and shit, the party got started. You couldn't tell my pregnant ass nothing as I dropped it down low to Beyonce's "Get Me Bodied". Mega still hasn't said shit to me, but he couldn't keep his eyes off me as I danced and laughed without a care in the world.

"You better sit ya ass down before you twerk my babies out!" Mega said standing in front of me. I honestly had nothing to say to him so I said nothing as I continued to dance like he wasn't there.

"So you just gonna act like I'm not even here!"

"You ain't acknowledge me either Jason so what the fuck!" I snapped.

"I'm sorry lil mama, I don't wanna argue no more," he said.

"You think I want to argue Jason?" I asked.

"Naw I know you don't, so can we make up?" he asked, grabbing my waist.

"You said some fucked up shit to me today," I said sadly.

"I was mad, you keep accusing me of shit I'm not doing."

"I'm sorry aight," I said, giving in.

"You love me lil mama?" he asked with a smile.

"Always," I said standing on my tippy toes to kiss his soft lips. We danced and hugged for a few songs before heading back to the V.I.P section. As soon as I was feeling better, and me and Mega were on good terms, I looked up only to see that bitch Jayda walk in.

"What the fuck is she doing here!" I snapped loud enough for everyone to here. As soon as I said it, Camille and the other girls looked to see who I was talking about.

"Uh huh, I know that ain't the bitch he got working for him is it?" Camille asked.

"Yup that's her, but what I'm trying to figure out is what she's doing here!" I snapped, looking at Mega.

"I invited her Cherish, chill the fuck out please!" he snapped before getting up and walking over to Jayda.

"Why the fuck would he invite her here?" Shana asked.

"I don't know, but imma find out!" I said fuming. When they walked over to us, she had the brightest smile on her face.

"Hey Cherish, I hope you don't mind, but Jason invited me," she said politely.

"Hello Jayda," I said rolling my eyes. I know she saw my attitude, but she completely ignored it.

"She looks so fucking familiar," Camille whispered.

"All I know is she's from Atlanta and she wants my man."

"I don't know where I know her from, but I know her, I promise you," Camille said with conviction.

"You look so beautiful," Jayda said to Camille with a smile.

"Thank you... What's your name again?" Camille asked with a smirk.

"And you Cherish, you're blowing up these days," she said looking at me with a fake smile.

"Bitch, did you just call her fat!" Camille snapped.

"No I didn't, I mean she is pregnant though."

"Why the fuck are you here!" I snapped.

"Because Jason invited me, maybe we can all go out sometime, shop, dinner, you know girls day out," she said with a smile.

"I don't know about them, but I don't need no more friends," Camille said seriously.

"Ummmm I'm good," I said.

"Y'all are being some mean girls right now and I don't understand why."

"We ain't being mean, just real," Shana said.

"Look, I know you're a little insecure Cherish, and I mean with your age I get it, but me and Mega are just friends," she said pissing me off.

"Ok, I can't do this fake shit no more, you gotta go!" Camille snapp

"What's the problem?" Mega asked walking up to us.

"This bitch is the problem!" Camille said.

"Don't think I didn't peep that you called him by his nickname, how the fuck would you know that!" I snapped.

"We work together. I'm around him very often, I know everything about him damn near," she said with a smirk.

"Aight, aight y'all chill. You gotta go Jayda, my bad shit went down like this," he said giving me and the girls the evil eyes, I could care less though.

Chapter Eight (Mega)

I wasn't sure why they ran Jayda away, but I knew it had something to do with me and that shit was fucked up. I watched as Jayda turned to leave with a sad look on her face, and in that moment, I felt fucked up that I had even put her in this situation.

"Yo, Jayda wait up," I said rushing to catch up to her. By the time I caught up to her, she was already out the club and almost to her car.

"Jason, just leave it alone," she said with teary eyes.

"Naw, I'm sorry they were acting that way, you didn't deserve that shit," I said honestly.

"I can't keep doing this Jason."

"Doing what?"

"All this time that we've been spending together. I like you, I think you are sweet and compassionate and just a good dude," she said. I watched as she poured her feelings out to me and as much as I didn't want to hurt her, I didn't feel the same way at all. Maybe if shit was different and I ain't meet lil mama, but honestly, Cherish is the only woman I really want.

"Jayda, I think you cool as shit, smart, funny, sexy as hell, but I don't…"

"Don't even say it."

"I'm with Cherish and I ain't leaving her, that's me just keeping it real."

"Ok, see you at work," she said sadly before getting into her car and pulling off. Damn, I knew she was attracted to me, but I didn't think she had real feelings for me. I knew I couldn't tell Cherish what happened because her first thought would be for me to fire Jayda, and I honestly didn't want to do that. Besides her having feelings for me, she is a good ass worker and she knows me, she knows my likes and dislikes, who knows when or if I would ever find a secretary or a fucking true friend like that. Walking back into the club, I went over to Cherish only to have her roll her eyes at me. I guess she was upset because I went to check on Jayda. But what the fuck, that's one of the reasons lil mama fell in love with me, because I'm a real nigga that genuinely cares and I ain't gonna say fuck Jayda after I'm the one that invited her.

"Stop being like that, you know y'all were wrong," I said shaking my head.

"What the fuck, you supposed to have my back. You didn't ask me what she did to make us snap, you just took her side!" Cherish snapped.

"Man, I know how Cam is."

"You know how I am too, and I ain't messy!"

"Here you go tryna argue again!" I said getting pissed.

"I'm not even tryna argue cuz it ain't worth it," she said getting up and walking away. After twenty minutes and no Cherish, I went looking for her only to have Camille tell me that she left. How the fuck she gonna leave without telling me. Finding out she had left pissed me off to the point that I didn't even want to be at the party no more. I was use to her being stubborn, but Goddamn she ain't giving a nigga no kind of slack. When I got home, she was lying in bed naked like usual. As soon as I saw her body, I wasn't mad no more, a nigga was tryna get deep into her pussy. After showering, I got in bed next to her. Gently grabbing a breast, I placed her nipple into my mouth and sucked her breast lightly.

"Hmmmmm damn," she moaned. Grabbing the back of my head, she pushed my head deeper into her breast, letting me know that she wanted me to suck harder. As I sucked her breast, I was surprised when I tasted her breast milk, and it didn't taste bad. Working my way from her breast to her stomach, I continued to leave traces of my lips on her body as she stirred in her sleep. Just recently, she started to be comfortable again with me sexually. A nigga was fiending for some of her sweet pussy, but I refused to move at a faster pace than her, so I told my dick to shut the fuck up and I waited patiently. When I got down to her neatly trimmed pussy, a nigga mouth started to water like a muthafucka, I had to catch myself from drooling. Licking her outer pussy lightly, I felt her jump, all while moaning for more. I don't know what happened, but when I began licking her she started squirming and locked my head in between her legs, all while screaming for me to get off of her.

"Nooooo I don't want to, get off me," she screamed while slapping me in the head.

"What the fuck Cherish stop!" I snapped trying to pull my head from in between her legs. When she finally let me go, she was crying hysterically.

"Cherish look at me, it's me lil mama!" I said trying to move her hands from her face. Finally realizing that it was just me, she ran into my arms and broke down even harder.

"I'm so sorry Jason," she said while crying.

"Shhhhh don't cry. You know I hate it when you cry."

"What is wrong with me?" she asked.

"You've been through a lot."

"Why are you even with me?"

"Because I love everything about you."

"I'm damaged goods; you can't even have sex with me without me acting crazy."

"That's why I said you should really speak to somebody."

"I made an appointment to talk to someone, I go next week," she said sadly. Grabbing her waist, I pulled her closely to me. Yeah a nigga needed some, but not this way. I wasn't gonna force her to do something she didn't want to.

"I don't want you scared of me Cherish, I would never hurt you."

"I'm not scared of you. I don't know, certain times you touch me, I flash back to those times with Caesar," she said completely pissing me off.

"So I remind you of that nigga?"

"Noooo, you don't remind me of him, I can't explain it."

"Naw, you did a real good fucking job explaining if you ask me!"

"Please stop, I don't want to fight, can you just hold me?" she asked with teary eyes. I held her until sleep took over her body. I ain't gonna lie, I was feeling fucked up that she would even compare my touch to that pervert ass rapist nigga. This shit was getting out of hand and if she didn't get help and get better, I wasn't sure how long I could deal with this.

Chapter Nine (Jayda)

I went in there trying to be nice to them hoes. Granted, it was only to get in good with Cherish, but that's beside the point. As soon as they saw me, they made it a point to make me feel unwanted and I wasn't feeling that shit. At the end of the day, I don't give a flying fuck about Cherish or her minions; my only concern is Jason Cruz. When I told him how I felt, I instantly knew from the look on his face that he felt the same way, but couldn't tell me because he didn't want to hurt Cherish. That bitch is a child and I guess since she's pregnant and he's such a good guy, he doesn't want to leave her. Shit, I grew up with no dad and I came out just fine, I say leave the bitch and get on this money team, but I can't fault him for being a good guy. Now I knew what I had to do, I had to get rid of that bitch that got him hooked. Once I do that, I know he'll be with me. Walking into work, I was surprised to see Jason already there; I usually beat him to the office.

"Hey boss man, what's up?" I asked.

"Nothing, you ready to get to work, we got a long day today," he said with his head in his hands. His clothes were a mess and he looked like he'd been drinking.

"I know something's wrong Jason," I said sitting beside him.

"Man, it's Cherish. She had a fucked up past and she bringing that shit into our relationship, I just don't know if I can keep dealing with it."

"You shouldn't have to. Now before you go and think I'm being a hater because I want you, that's not the case. I see you love

Cherish, but is she really old enough for the type of love you're looking for?" I said honestly.

"You think I'm holding her back?"

"I mean she looks to be what, eighteen, and she's already pregnant and playing step mommy, plus you said she had a horrible past, so she never really had a childhood."

"Maybe you're right, which is why I plan on helping her with the kids, getting a nanny so she can still have a life outside of us and the kids. I don't know if we will work out, but I know I ain't gonna throw the towel in, I don't know why I'm even tripping," he said flipping the script.

"Well whatever you decide, I got ya back," I forced myself to say. I thought maybe I could play off his emotions, but that didn't even work. I don't know what her young ass did to this nigga, but he wasn't going nowhere.

"So where is Cherish now?" I asked.

"She should be home," he said.

"Oh ok. Well call her and let her know you were thinking of her, we women like that sort of shit," I said with a laugh. Picking up the office phone, he dialed her number, and when she answered, he had the biggest smile on his face.

"Stop eating all them pickles," he said before I walked out. I couldn't handle my man talking to her ass. After a few hours of work, it was time for my break and I couldn't be any more amped as I walked into his office to tell him I would be leaving.

"Hey Jason, I have to make a run, but I will be back before my break is over."

"You don't have to come back, I'm taking Cherish to her doctor's appointment and I'll be spending the rest of the day with her. Have a good day Jayda," he said before I headed out. Hopping in my car, I drove to the house Jason and Cherish shared, and sure enough, her car was parked in the garage. Parking down the street, I threw on some sneakers I kept in the car and jogged up the street to their house. Looking at her nice little Benz pissed me off. Here I was almost twenty-five years old and I ain't never drove a fucking car that nice and her young ass got one handed to her, pussy must be made of gold. Pulling out my keys, I scratched little lines all over the driver's side of her car. When I was done, I went back to my car with a smile on my face. If I couldn't have his ass, and I couldn't get rid of the bitch that had him, then I would at least have my fun with her. On the way home, an idea popped into my head that would top all this shit. As soon as I got home, I rushed inside to talk to Ashley.

"Bitch, I need a favor!"

"What's up, you got that sneaky look on ya face, so I know it's good," she said with a smirk. Giving her the rundown of exactly what I wanted for her to do, her eyes were wide, and her mouth had dropped down to the floor.

"Bitch you scandalous!" she said, laughing loudly.

"I don't give a fuck!"

"So you doing all this for a nigga that don't want you?"

"He does want me, but if you don't want to do it, I'll get somebody else to," I said with an attitude.

"Cut it out, you know I got you. I can get one of my boo's to do it, but I'm just saying, why go through all this, you a bad bitch and you can get any nigga."

"I don't want any nigga, I want him."

"Alright then."

"See that's why I love you!" I said kissing her passionately. See I knew she was in love with me, but all I saw her as was a friend and somebody who would do anything for me.

Chapter Ten (Cherish)

Things with me and Mega have been weird as hell since the night of Camille's party. I tried to explain to him exactly what I meant and that I wasn't trying to compare him to my step dad, but he wasn't trying to hear that. We have been so distant with each other that it's starting to feel like we're roommates instead of lovers. I don't want to push him away with all my baggage, which is why today I'm seeing the therapist in hopes that she can help me get better. I haven't been driving my car because Mega's ass been so over protective lately, so I had to wait for Camille to come pick me up.

"Mega, you seen my studs?" I asked as I searched the house for my favorite earrings. I couldn't find them anywhere and it was pissing me off, they belonged to my granny and everybody knew how much they meant to me.

"Naw did you check your jewelry box?" Mega asked.

"I looked everywhere, I can't find it!"

"Calm down Cherish, I'll check your car damn!" he snapped back.

"I'll check it myself!" I snapped before stomping to my car. Today just wasn't my day. These babies got me having the worst heartburn known to man. I stayed up last night because it felt like they were having a party in my stomach. I ate pickles all night and been farting since I woke up. Whoever said pregnancy was awesome, or them bitches walking around in high heels and shit, let me be the one to say that shit is a lie. I was miserable and taking all of it out on Jason, I didn't mean to, but I was.

"Oh my God, Megaaaaaa!" I screamed from outside.

"What's wrong!" he said as he came running out of the house in nothing but a towel.

"Look at my car!" I snapped on the verge of tears. I couldn't believe someone had the nerve to do some shit like this. I don't bother anybody, so I needed answers.

"Damn, that shit fucked up," Mega said with his fist to his mouth.

"I know it's fucked up you ain't gotta say it, but what I need to know is who the fuck did it and why!"

"Man, it was probably some bad ass kid around here," he said, blowing it off. True, although where we lived was a suburban good neighborhood, it was filled with children and they have been known to do things like ring your doorbell and run, but I have never known them to do some shit like this. This right here was some bitch shit that a grown ass petty bitch would do. I couldn't even come to terms with what I was looking at.

"Jason, you are usually a smart man, so please tell me why you think some damn kids would key my car!"

"Why the fuck you making it into a big deal like I ain't gonna have it fixed by later, you don't even drive the shit!"

"I don't give a fuck if you could magically fix it, this is my car and I don't appreciate somebody fucking with it!" I screamed. For him, it didn't mean anything because he was use to having shit. Me, I appreciated everything I had, every meal I ate and everything I owned.

"I know babe calm down, I really think you're just being paranoid. When is your appointment?"

"Don't talk to me like I'm some crazy person imagining shit, Mega, don't do that. I'm going today and you're ass ain't taking me!"

"Why the fuck you acting like this, and why didn't you tell me it was today? You got me out here acting a fool in a towel!"

"Well take ya ass inside!" I said, walking into the house.

"Yo, you being real fucking childish!"

"I am seventeen so..."

"You know what, I ain't doing this dumb shit with you!" he said, walking into his closet to get dressed. Sitting at the edge of the bed, I kind of felt bad for snapping on him, but I wasn't gonna tell him that. Maybe it was childish of me, I don't know, but right now I don't even care.

"I'm out!" he screamed before starting to walk out the room door.

"So that's how you gonna be?" I asked, pouting my lips.

"Man what!"

"No hug, no kiss, no I love you."

"My bad lil mama, you just make a nigga mad as hell sometimes," he said kissing my lips softly.

"I know, but I don't mean to," I said wrapping my arms around his waist.

"I love you," he said before heading out the room.

"I love you too!" I screamed. When he left, I finished getting ready and called Camille.

"Hey boo, I will be there in about five minutes," Camille said when she answered.

"Alright I'll be outside waiting," I said before hanging up. When I got outside, I didn't even want to look at my car because it pissed me off just to see it. Standing outside, I scrolled through my newsfeed on Facebook while waiting for Camille's late ass. Remembering that I wanted to check the car for my granny's studs, I walked to unlock my car door. As I was bent over the driver's seat looking through my car, I felt strong hands yank me out.

"What the fuck!" I screamed, only to be met with a masked man.

"Shut the fuck up!" he said yoking me up.

"I got money, you can have it all!" I screamed, scrambling to hand him my purse.

"Didn't I say shut the fuck up!" he said while trying to drag me to his truck where a driver was waiting.

"Why you taking me? I said you can have everything I got, just don't hurt me, I'm pregnant," I said as tears fell from my eyes. I noticed a sympathetic look in his eyes and decided to try my luck.

"Please, you're gonna hurt my babies, you don't have to do this!" I said while he continued to drag me. I wasn't gonna let anybody hurt my babies, so I wasn't getting in that truck without a fight. Getting frustrated with me, he put his gun to my head and through gritted teeth told me to stop fighting him. After killing my mom, my step-dad and my friends, I thought that life would get normal for me; I didn't understand why everybody was out to get me. While walking to the car, a series of gunshots rang out, causing the masked man to let me go. Rushing down to the ground, I protected my stomach to the best of my ability. I watched as the masked man hopped into the truck and the driver pulled off quickly.

"Oh my God, Cherish, are you ok?" Camille asked, helping me up. I couldn't even say anything, I was in complete shock.

"Who were them niggas?" she asked.

"I don't know," I said through tears. Pulling out her phone, Camille called Mark and Mega, and in no time, they were at the house.

"Are you ok?"

"I'm so tired of this shit Mega, why can't I be happy?" I said as my body shook.

"Maybe she needs to go to the hospital," Mark said with a worried face. Picking me up, Mega took me to the car, gently placing me in the back seat. When we got to the hospital, I was taken back and examined quickly, and not one time did Mega let go of my hand. The nurse strapped me to a machine to check the babies heartbeat.

"The babies seem to be fine and in no distress, but your blood pressure is through the roof," the doctor said as soon as he walked in.

"So what do we do, how can you treat this?" Mega asked.

"She needs to be put on bed rest, I don't want her doing anything strenuous," the doctor said.

"You hear him, so that means chill out and stay in bed."

"I am not staying in bed, he said strenuous activity, which means heavy lifting and stuff like that," I said.

"That also mean no stressing mentally or physically," the doctor corrected.

"Ok, I can do that," I said rubbing my belly.

"Good, now I don't think there is any reason why you can't be released right now, so I will print out your release form," he said before walking out.

"Did you recognize them niggas?" Mega asked while grinding his teeth, something he always did when he was upset.

"No, they had mask on."

"How many?"

"Two, one driving and the one that grabbed me."

"Did they say anything?"

"No, I tried to give him my purse, but he didn't want it, he wanted to take me," I said as tears fell from my face.

"I don't understand why the fuck somebody would try and take you, but imma find out."

"Please, just leave it alone."

"I can't do that, but until I do find out what's going on, I need for you to be cautious. Don't leave the house without someone with you and when you're home, keep the alarm on."

"Ok Jason," I said. When we finally got home, Mega was out the door in a hurry. He left Camille to stay with me and even hired somebody to keep watch outside; he really wasn't playing no games when it came to me and his babies. Me and Camille laid on the bed in the guest room on some Netflix and chill type shit; we were having a good time. I actually felt better after what happened today, that is, until there was a knock at the door.

"Somebody supposed to be coming?" Camille asked.

"I don't think so," I said with a scared face.

"Girl, don't be scared. I got my baby on me and we ain't playin no games," she said, pulling her gun out of her purse. When we walked up to the door, we weren't expecting to see who we saw on the other side. I thought shit couldn't get any worse, but it could.

Chapter Eleven (Jayda)

"What the fuck kind of fuck boys did you get to do this!" I snapped at Ashley.

"They said some bitch came and was busting like a nigga."

"I don't wanna hear that shit, why didn't they shoot back? Shit, or they could have shot Cherish's ass, I would have been ok with that."

"You really want that girl dead, Jayda?" she asked.

"I don't give a fuck what happens to her, I just want her gone!"

"I think you taking this shit too far, I'm all for you getting ya man, but damn."

"I asked you to do one simple fucking thing, just one thing!"

"Bitch don't be mad at me, shit you asked me to get somebody and I did that, you just mad cuz shit got all fucked up!" she snapped at me. I had some fucking words for her ass, but before I could speak, my phone started ringing.

"Hello?" I answered.

"Hey Jay, it's me Mega, I need you to handle shit, I'm taking some days off."

"Ok, but is everything alright."

"Naw, some niggas attacked Cherish."

"Oh my God, is she ok, are the babies good?" I asked, praying that he said they were at least dead.

"They're fine and so is Cherish," he said.

"Thank God, imma go check on her, just make sure she's ok," I said.

"Naw, I don't think that's a good idea."

"I know she doesn't really like me, but I wanna check on her."

"I appreciate that Jayda, but I don't know."

"I will go and make sure she knows that you didn't send me," I said.

"Aight that's cool," he said before hanging up. Hopping up, I made sure I looked flawless before heading out the door. When I pulled up in front of their house, there was a fucking bodyguard standing outside the door, like come on now, it ain't even that serious, fuck her.

"Hi I'm Jayda, I'm here to see Cherish," I said.

"Go ahead and knock," the guard said. Knocking on the door, I waited for someone to answer. I knew when she came to the door she would surprised, and that's exactly what I wanted.

"Jayda, what are you doing here?" she asked when she opened the door.

"Jason told me what happened and I just came to check on you."

"Ummmm ok, well you checked," she said smartly.

"Can I come in?" I asked her rude ass.

"I know you from somewhere, what school did you go to?" Camille said from behind her. She continued to stare at me with curious eyes

"I went to school in LA!" I said rolling my eyes at Camille. If there was anything I hated most, it was a nosey ass bitch, and that was Camille.

"Look, I know you don't like me, but I really just wanted to make sure you were ok," I said.

"I appreciate you coming Jayda, I really do, but let's keep it real for just a minute, you and I both know you want my man, so knock it off. I'm good, the babies are good and you can go!" she said, slamming the door in my face. That ignorant bitch, I swear I don't know how Jason tolerates her ass because I would have been slapped the shit out of her. Getting back into my car, I pulled off feeling like I didn't accomplish shit. I didn't even get to come inside to check it out. When I arrived to my house, I walked in only to be met by the biggest blow to my face.

"What the fuck!" I screamed, holding my face.

"Where the fuck is our money!" a man said holding a gun in my face.

"Nigga, I don't even know you!" I snapped.

"Yeah, but this bitch do," he said, moving out the way showing me a badly beaten Ashley.

"What the fuck is going on Ash?" I asked.

"This the nigga I got to kidnap Cherish," she said through tears.

"You didn't even kidnap her right, but you at my fucking crib drawing guns and hitting bitches, all for money you don't deserve," I said spitting blood out my mouth.

"Fuck all that, how was I supposed to know that some crazy bitch would show up busting?"

"I don't know, but that ain't my problem!" I snapped.

"You got a smart fucking mouth!" he said looking at me seductively.

"Oh yeah, you tryna do something about it?"

"I got a few things in mind," he said with a smirk before hitting me in the face with the butt of his gun. I wasn't gonna let this nigga keep putting his fucking hands on me, that's some shit I refused to tolerate. He will not be scarring up this money making face. Jumping up, I punched him dead in his face. I wasn't no bitch and the worse thing a nigga could ever do is underestimate me. Standing in a fighting stance, I proceeded to deliver him an ass whooping his mama should've gave his ass as a child.

"Nigga you don't be hitting no fucking women, bitch ass!" I said before kicking him in the face.

"And your stupid ass, how the fuck he know where we live!" I snapped at Ashley before snatching the gun out of the dude's hand.

"I'm sorry, damn. I didn't think he would do no shit like this!"

"That's where you fucked up at, leave the thinking to me!" I said before dragging his body out of my fucking apartment. I didn't give a shit who found him, who helped him or if his ass died, as long as he wasn't in my shit waving that gun. After getting in the shower, I examined my face, he didn't do shit that makeup couldn't cover up, and for that I was thankful.

"I'm sorry Jayda," Ashley said sitting beside me on the bed.

"Naw it ain't your fault, if I want something done right, I need to do it myself."

"This shit getting heavy, maybe we should just go back to Atlanta, shit was good there."

"Why did you come if shit was so good there?"

"I love you and I wanted to be wherever you were," she said, feeding me bullshit.

"So it has nothing to do with all them robberies you pulled on them niggas? It didn't have shit to do with them niggas coming after you!" I snapped.

"How you know that?" her dumb ass asked.

"I make it my business to know everything, and I don't appreciate you tryna play me."

"I never said I didn't come for more than one reason, but my love for you was the biggest reason."

"Yeah aight, well I ain't going back without my man."

Chapter Twelve (Mega)

It's been a month since they tried to kidnap Cherish, and to be honest, she isn't doing good. I have to force her to eat and she hasn't been outside since. She doesn't check the mail, she won't meet Jasmine at the bus stop, she won't do anything that has to do with stepping out the front door. I'm not a doctor, I'm not equipped to handle these kinds of problems and I don't know how to help her other than to catch the niggas that did this shit. I had no choice but to go back to work, I got people that depend on me, and I can't leave it up to Jayda to get it done. Niggas don't know her like that and don't trust her to do what I do for their careers. Getting dressed, I watched as Cherish laid in bed crying, this shit couldn't be healthy for the babies. I have a doctor that was willing to do house visits, and he says she's in a deep depression. He suggested that someone stay with her at all times. I don't think she would do anything to harm herself and our babies, but to be on the safe side, I have Camille coming and hopefully she can get her out of this slump. Pulling the covers from over her, she yanked them back.

"I love you lil mama," I said kissing her cheek. She didn't even say it back, she just continued to cry. Looking at her one last time, I turned around and walked out the room to wait for Camille. Hearing a knock at the door, I got up to open it.

"Hey, Mega how is she?"

"Not good, I've never seen someone cry everyday and every night."

"Is she eating?"

"Not really, and she won't say anything to me," I said sadly. I wasn't no bitch nigga, but this shit right here was fucking me up mentally. I loved her with all my heart and to see her in so much emotional pain was heart breaking.

"I don't understand. She was good when I left her that night, I don't know what happened, but imma find out."

"Thanks Cam," I said hugging her.

"You good. I called her therapist and she is going to come here tomorrow."

"I appreciate it," I said. We talked for a little longer before I headed to the office. When I got there, I was actually happy to be here instead of home and that wasn't a good look.

"Hey Jason!" Jayda said running up and hugging me.

"Hey Jay, how you been?" I asked.

"I've been good, but how are you and Cherish?"

"Man, shit bad!" I said shaking my head.

"Damn, I'm sorry," she replied.

"It's cool, let's get to work, take my mind off the at home shit."

"Aight, boss man," she said. While catching up on paperwork, I couldn't get Cherish off my mind, I was worried about her.

"Ummmm some police are out here for you," Jayda said from the intercom.

"Send them in."

"Hello Mr. Cruz, I'm Detective Davis."

"What's this about?"

"This is about Cherish Daniels."

"Is she ok!" I asked, jumping up.

"Oh no no she's fine, but we are trying to locate her, we have some news about her mother."

"If it's something bad, she can't handle it right now," I said shutting him down.

"I don't understand."

"She's pregnant with twins and suffering from depression, if this is bad news, it needs to wait."

"I understand, here's my card, have her give me a call when she's up to it," he said.

"Thank you for being sympathetic," I said.

"No problem. Was she close to her mother?" he asked before leaving.

"No, her mother abused her severely before meeting me. She ran away and never looked back," I lied.

"Oh, I'm sorry to hear that. Well you have a good day," he said before leaving.

"Is everything ok?" Jayda asked.

"Yeah everything's straight, if it ain't one thing it's another," I said, stressed the fuck out.

"Here, let me help you," she said standing behind me. She began to massage my shoulders and I would be lying if I said that shit didn't feel good as hell.

"Damn…" I said.

"You're so stiff, that comes from stress Jason."

"Well, I got a lot of shit to stress about."

"Well not when you're with me, so relax, I got you."

Chapter Thirteen (Cherish)

I don't know how this happened, one minute I was ok, and the next I couldn't get out of bed or stop crying. Sometimes I think I'm feeling better and I want to get out of bed and interact with Jasmine, but when I try, the tears start falling and I can't control it. When I think about all that I've been through it makes my heart hurt, literally. I feel this unbearable pain in my chest. I know I have these babies inside me that I have to be strong for, but I'm so tired of fighting and being strong. I was strong with my mom's abuse, I was a fighter when I bounced back from Caesar and his perverted ways, but now my past and what they did is haunting me. When I close my eyes, I see them in my nightmares. Even from the grave, they won't let me be happy.

"Hey boo, how are you?" I heard Camille's voice say. Ignoring her, I just stayed under the cover, hoping that she would get the hint and leave.

"Cherish, I know you hear me talking to you!" she screamed before yanking the covers back.

"Get out Camille, damn!"

"No, I ain't leaving unless your ass is back to normal!" she said opening the curtains to my room.

"Why you coming in here taking over shit!"

"Girl, it's dark as hell in here, you living like a fucking vampire. What you melt if you get some sunlight? Ya ass stinks to high hell and ya fucking hair look like some crows been picking at the shit, hell probably vultures thinking ya ass dead!"

"Fuck you!"

"No fuck you for letting them muthafuckas win. You think them niggas that tried to kidnap you are thinking bout ya ass, you think ya mama and step daddy nasty asses thinking good thoughts about you from hell? Fuck no, they smiling cause you spiraling out of fucking control. What about Meeka and Tyree with their shiesty asses? You letting all these people win."

"I'm tired Cam damn, I'm tired of fighting and being strong. I'm so tired of people tryna hurt me, what did I ever do to anybody but be a good person!"

"You ain't did shit, you had it bad boo, but so did my best friend Shante. Granted, she didn't have it as bad as you did, but she didn't let it keep her down and neither should you."

"Well maybe I'm not as strong as Shante. I feel like God played a trick on me, he gave me just enough to think maybe my life was changing, maybe I would be happy, then he snatched that shit and replaced it with the same old drama."

"You can't go blaming God; you are the strongest person I know. Come on, you can't let this defeat you."

"I don't know what's wrong with me. I don't feel like moving, I don't feel like living."

"You talking crazy, you got people here that love you, babies that didn't ask to be created, it's your job to give them the love you didn't get!"

"What if I'm not a good mom?" I asked lowly. I never told anybody that I'd been having these thoughts, but I was.

"Why wouldn't you be a good mom? You are a great parent to Jasmine, my kids love you to the end, you are kind and loving, what would make you think some shit like that?"

"I don't want to end up like my mom," I said through tears.

"You're not your mom's crazy ass, you are Cherish muthafucking Daniels!" she screamed.

"You're right," I said before going to hug her.

"Uh huh bitch, you need to hop in the shower and wash that funky kitty kat several times before you can even come near me!" she snapped, causing me to burst out laughing.

"How is Mega?" I asked while running the shower.

"He's worried about you, and I honestly think he feels defeated."

"I don't want to lose him Cam."

"You won't, but you need to go get ya man," she said. Hopping in the shower, I couldn't believe that I was that depressed that I stopped washing my ass. I stayed in the shower for over an hour before finally feeling clean enough. When I got out the shower, tossing my hair in a ponytail, I threw on some black maternity jeans, a black and white Polo shirt, my black Jordan's and I was ready to go.

"Thank you boo," I said hugging Camille tight.

"You would have done it for me, now go ahead and get your man. Oh and you got an appointment for the therapist tomorrow, but I will call her and let her know you will be coming into the office," she said. Hopping in my car, I adjusted my seat to fit my belly and pulled off on a mission. Stopping by the Cheesecake Factory, I ordered Mega his favorite meal. My next stop was to get him some flowers and a card. Yeah I know men don't like that kind of stuff, but I just wanted to thank him for putting up with me. Pulling up to his office, I waved to the security guard and kept it pushing to the elevator. Walking pass Jayda's desk, she wasn't there and I was glad that she wasn't, I couldn't stand the sight of her ass. Stepping inside Mega's office, I wasn't prepared for what I saw.

"Hey babe!" I said holding the balloons, flowers, card and food, only to find him sitting at his desk with Jayda on top of it in front of him rubbing his shoulders. No they weren't fucking, or kissing, but they should have been. Dropping everything I had in my hands, I charged that bitch, slapping her across the face. I was about to tear her ass up until Mega grabbed me.

"Get the fuck off me, don't touch me!" I screamed.

"It's not what you think!"

"I think that bitch was between ya legs, rubbing you like she was ya woman!"

"I know and I'm sorry, but nothing happened, I didn't fuck her!"

"You should've fucked her, cuz the way I'm feeling, it's just as bad!" I said before slapping him in the face.

"Don't fucking put ya hands on him bitch!"

"You so fucking stupid bitch. He don't want you, and even with me gone, it will never be you. But you know what, you can have him and learn the shit for ya self," I said pulling as much spit and mucus that I could and spitting dead in that bitch's face before heading for the elevators. With tears clouding my vision, I rushed to my car and pulled off. Grabbing my phone, I was about to call Camille, but changed my mind. When I pulled up to the house I shared with the love of my life, the tears started falling again. How could I be so fucking stupid? Hopping out the car, I rushed to pack my shit. I knew Mega, so I knew he wasn't far behind me so I needed to hurry. Grabbing a piece of paper, I prepared to write him a letter. I knew it was messy and maybe I should have told him this in person, but the way my love for him was set up, as soon as he said sorry I would fall into his arms. Placing the note on the nightstand, I put my bags in my car and I drove away without looking back. My first stop was to Camille's house. Knocking on the door, I waited for her to answer. When she came to the door, I fell into her arms.

"What happened boo!" she asked with a scared look. When I ran the story down to her, she was pissed off, just like I knew she would be.

"I packed my shit and left. If he wants that bitch, he can have her!"

"I'm supporting you in whatever you choose, but I don't think you should leave him forever. Yeah he needs to be taught a lesson, but he didn't even sleep with the chick, so really he didn't cheat."

"He cheated emotionally which is way worse. If you would have seen them Camille, oooohhhh I swear to God I wanted to kill them!"

"Don't worry, you can stay here," she said hugging me.

"No, I'm getting my own place, shit I got the money for it."

"So you really done?"

"I don't know, but what I do know is I love him and I don't see myself with anyone but him," I said with teary eyes.

"So do you think he has feelings for her?"

"I don't know Cam. I feel like she knows him better than me, seeing them interact the way that they were hurt me to the core."

"Did you tell him that?"

"No, I just packed my shit and left, but I did write a letter."

"I'm so sorry," she said hugging me.

"It's fine. I love Jason and I hope we end up together forever, but until then, I'm going to work on myself and getting better for Jasmine and the babies."

"Damn, so what about Jas?"

"What you mean? I love that little girl, and just because me and Mega are going through this, I'm not taking it out on her. Maybe I won't be able to tuck her in at night, but I will damn sure be seeing her often."

"Awwwww that is so fucking sweet."

"Shut up," I laughed. Honestly, I didn't feel as bad as I thought I would leaving Mega. Of course, I was gonna miss him, but I was more focused on being a better me and if leaving him was what I needed to do to start that process, I was all for it.

Chapter Fourteen (Mega)

"What the fuck did I do!" I snapped while pacing back and forth in my office. I wanted to go after her and try to explain, but honestly, what would I say.

"You ain't do nothing wrong," Jayda said with a smile, while rubbing my arm.

"Yo, no disrespect, but imma need for you to back the fuck up!" I said grabbing my shit to go home.

"Where you going?"

"I'm going to try and stop lil mama from leaving a nigga," I said walking out. Hopping in my car, I sped home. When I got there, Cherish's car wasn't there, which I was hopping meant that I'd beat her home. Walking into our house, I looked around. Checking the closet, I noticed a lot of her things were gone, a nigga was fucked up. Grabbing my phone, I called her over and over only for it to go straight to voicemail. As I paced our bedroom floor, my eyes fell onto a note on the nightstand.

Mega,

How dare you hurt me after everything that I've been through. How dare you make me seem like a crazy person when I told you that she wanted you and how dare you put me in such a fucked up situation. I'm pregnant with your children. While I'm sitting home dealing with depression and second guessing myself, you were out building an emotional relationship with someone else. I understand that shit with us has become difficult, which is why I came up to your office to apologize and thank you for sticking with me. Before I met you, I didn't think I would ever find someone that could love me wholeheartedly without wanting anything in return. You saved me, and for that, I will forever be grateful and I will forever see you as a loving and kindhearted man, but I refuse to compete with another woman or be cheated on. I've let so many people walk all over me and treat me how they saw fit and I refuse to do that with you. I expected more, maybe I set the bar too high, maybe I expected too much from you, and for that, I'm the stupid one. I love you more than I love life itself, my world revolves around you and Jasmine, always has, but I see now that my love was taken for granted. I see now that as much as I love you, maybe you aren't ready to love me the same in return. I am leaving you, as much as I don't want to, I know it's for the best. I am going to learn to love myself, dedicate all the love and effort that I once gave you to myself.

Love Always Your lil mama

She left me; I couldn't believe she actually left me. Picking up the nightstand, I threw it across the room. Knocking everything off the dresser, I screamed a gut wrenching scream. Damn, I know I fucked up, but I never thought she would leave me. I didn't sleep with the chick and my connection with Jayda was nowhere near close to the connection I shared with Cherish.

The look on her face when she walked in my office hurt my soul. To know that I was the reason for her tears and pain made me feel like shit. How was I gonna explain this shit to Jasmine, her night isn't complete if she doesn't see Cherish before going to sleep. As I stood in the middle of the room I once shared with lil mama, I felt something wet on my face. Wiping my face, I realized that they were tears, real tears. I haven't truly shed a tear since the loss of my parents, and now I've cried more than once over Cherish. After getting myself together, I grabbed my keys and headed out to meet Jasmine at the bus stop. When she got into my car, I wasn't surprised when the first thing out her mouth was her asking where Cherish was.

"But we always get our nails done on Friday," she pouted.

"I'm sorry baby girl."

"It's ok, I'm sure she'll make it up to me," she said with a smile. When we got back to the house, I was surprised to see Camille's car parked outside my house. Hopping out the car, I rushed to the door to meet her.

"Where's Cherish?"

"Boy bye, I'm here to pick up Jasmine, not answer your questions."

"Hey Auntie Cam!" Jasmine screamed excitedly.

"Hey baby, you ready to get your nails done!" she said, but not before rolling her eyes at me.

"Jas go pack your overnight bag," I said. When she was out of earshot, I plead my case to Camille.

"Uh huh nigga, don't even try it," she said, putting her hand in my face.

"Yo I fucked up, I know that, but you of all people know how much I love Cherish. I can't handle her leaving me."

"Mega you were fucking wrong and you don't deserve her, so miss me with the pity party!"

"I just need to talk to her."

"She doesn't want to talk to you."

"I just want to apologize, please Cam."

"I don't know what to tell you, Jason."

"I just need you to help me out, damn."

"Honestly, I helped you out the first time you fucked up because I knew how much you loved her. Yeah I know she went through her shit and it had to have been hard on you, but did your selfish ass even think about Cherish and all that she'd been through. She was raped, beaten, made into an instant mommy, found out she was pregnant *with twins*, and then was almost kidnapped at gunpoint. She needed you, she needed your love and support, and you gave that, but you also emotionally built a relationship with someone else. Someone Cherish knew wanted you, someone older than her, more developed than her, do you know how that made her feel!" Camille snapped.

"Probably like shit," I said, feeling fucked up.

"Naw worse than that. You made her feel stupid, unworthy and unwanted. Feelings she has had to feel all her fucking life, and she never expected to feel that way with you!"

"I fucked up bad, but does this one time control all the good times, all the times I had her back and loved her."

"Nope, it doesn't, which is why I'm rooting for you to get her back, but I ain't helping you," she said. When Jasmine came downstairs, her and Camille headed out. Grabbing a bottle of Patron, I sat on the couch and started getting fucked up, I don't know how or when I was gonna get her back, but I wasn't gonna stop trying.

Chapter Fifteen (Cherish)

I've been at Camille's house for three days, and I'm ready to get the hell out of there. Don't get me wrong, I love Camille and Mark, but I need my own space. Almost every night I hear them having sex, and believe it or not, Mark is the screamer, which is just hilarious to me. Honestly, I just feel like I've worn out my welcome, which is why me and Camille were at Applebee's meeting with a realtor.

"So you sure this is what you want to do?" Camille asked.

"Yeah, I'm sure. I meet with the therapist next week. I have a plan for how I want and need for my life to be before I bring these babies into the world and I don't need Mega's ass distracting me."

"You miss him?"

"Is the sky blue... Hell yeah I miss my man," I said with a laugh.

"What you doing after we see a few houses?"

"I gotta pick up Jasmine from Mama Betty's house."

"Hello Ms. Daniels," the realtor I met online said as he walked up to the table. I didn't do white chocolate, but damn he was fine. Standing at about 6'0, nice build with his crisp suit on, not to mention, when he shook my hand I couldn't help but notice the tattoo on it.

"Hello, you must be Peter."

"Girl he fine," Camille said a little too loud.

"Don't mind her, have a seat."

"Ok, so tell me exactly what you're looking for."

"Well wherever I go won't be permanent, but I will be staying for the remainder of my pregnancy."

"So a furnished, month to month, two bedroom…"

"Yes, and a girl's room for my nine year old daughter."

"Oh wow, ok," he said surprised.

"Wow what?"

"You have a nine year old daughter, you look so young."

"Well thank you," I said with a smile. I never told people that Jasmine was my stepdaughter, even though most people looked at me like a freak when they found out my age, but whatever.

"No problem. Now that I have a better idea of what you're looking for, I think I have the perfect spot for you."

"Well shit, let's check it out!" Camille said hyped as hell. When we arrived at the condo, I instantly fell in love. He must have been really good at his job for him to have literally picked the perfect place for me. It wasn't too far from Mega and

Jasmine, but in the cut enough where I could have privacy and not risk him seeing me.

"This is beautiful!" I said as I walked through the home.

"I'm glad you like it."

"So it would be going in her name," I said pointing to Camille.

"But you'll be living here?"

"Yeah, I'm willing to pay in advance for my time here, so that wouldn't be an issue, I'm quiet, I have no friends and no man," I said pleading my case.

"Damn girl so what am I, chopped liver!"

"Oh hush, you know what I mean."

"I'm sure you won't be a problem," he said with a smile before pulling out the paperwork for Camille to sign. After paying the rent for five months in advance, we headed out and I was excited to be having a new start, excited to be on the road of independence. I love Mega, and I know he takes care of me, but there's nothing like being able to take care of yourself.

"Cherish?" the realtor called out to me before I could get into the car.

"Did I forget anything?" I asked.

"No, I just wanted you to know that I think you're beautiful and I would love to take you out sometime," he said catching me off guard.

"That's so sweet and I appreciate the offer, but I'm going to have no decline. Although I'm taking a break from my boyfriend, I would be lying if I said I was anywhere near over him."

"Well it was worth a try, right?" he said with a smirk, causing me to laugh out loud.

"Yes, you never know if you don't ask."

"Here, take my card in case you change your mind," he said reaching into his pocket and handing me his card. Hopping into his Benz, he pulled off leaving me feeling very wanted.

"Girl what he say," Camille asked as soon as I got into the car.

"He asked me out," I said blushing.

"So when is the date?" she asked.

"I turned him down. I love Mega, plus, I'm pregnant as hell."

"That ain't never stopped nobody, you ain't fucking him, you just going on a date."

"I don't know, maybe we can be friends, but nothing more."

"That's all you need to get that nigga jealous."

"I don't feel right using him like that, he seems nice."

"Alright, you go head and be lonely while Mega doing who knows what."

"You so fucking messy, you don't know if he doing anything, you just mad at him for hurting me," I said with a smirk.

"You damn right. I ain't feeling that nigga right now at all," she said laughing, but dead ass serious.

"I'm bout to start dinner, do my god babies want something specific?" she asked. This was another reason why I was ready to go. I loved cooking and had been learning new things every day, but Camille wanted to pamper me and didn't want for me to have to cook, so she did. Her food was bland and horrible. Sometimes it was so nasty that I would fake being sick and sneak out to McDonalds. I didn't want to hurt her feelings, and I appreciated her for letting me stay here, but something had to give.

"What you making?"

"Meatloaf, mashed potatoes and corn."

"That sounds good."

"Aight then," she said walking into the kitchen to start her dinner. Going into the guest room, I grabbed my laptop and began to shop for my new place. I was excited as hell to be furnishing my first apartment. After I was done, I logged into my Facebook, and the first page I went to was Mega's to see if he had been talking to any women. I know I left him, and I doubt he'll wait forever, but the thought of him giving what he gave to me to someone else was sickening to me. I laid in bed thinking about the shit that went down and whether or not he had feelings for Jayda. Did he love her like he loved me; did he see a future with her? Grabbing my purse, I searched for the realtor's card. When I found it, I grabbed my phone and sent him a text. I didn't have to wait hours for him to text back. As soon as I said who I was, he called me and we talked for literally four hours non-stop, until my phone died. He was sweet and nice and he showed me attention, maybe a date wouldn't hurt. As I continued to be in my thoughts, sleep took over my body and I welcomed it with open arms.

Today I see the therapist for the first time, and to say I'm nervous would be an understatement. It's times like this where I miss Mega so much. He's been calling and texting me nonstop and I haven't replied, He even went as far as to write an apology post on Facebook and tag me in it. Got everybody on Facebook talking bout "awwwwww" and "Oh just forgive him he loves you!" I wasn't paying any of them messages or comments any mind. What I miss about him is how he was always supportive and there for me whenever I needed him, and I needed him today. Pulling up to the address, I parked and wobbled into the building. Sitting in the waiting room, I waited to be called while looking through my phone. Opening a text message just sent to me, I smiled as I read it.

Hubby: Hey lil mama, I heard ya appointment is today and I just want you to know that you can do this, you are strong and brave and telling your story to this lady (or nigga) can do no harm. Only good can come from this, don't forget you are doing this to become a better you!! Love you and call me if you need me.

"Cherish Daniels," somebody said pulling me out of my thoughts. Wiping my eyes quickly, I popped up and headed back into the office.

"Have a seat Cherish," she said nicely.

"Thanks, this feels so weird."

"Why?"

"I guess because of all the movies I've seen with couches that look just like this. I'm supposed to lay back, tell you my problems and what you fix them," I said speaking honestly.

"Girl, I'm no genie, I don't grant wishes, and I'm no magician, I can't magically make problems disappear, but what I can do is help you to fix your problems," she said with a smile. She seemed cool. She was a beautiful chocolate woman like myself, and seemed to be in her early forties.

"Ok, I can handle that."

"Let's start with the basics, why are you here?"

"I'm here for a lot of reasons, but mainly because of my children. I want to be a better, healthier me for them," I said rubbing my belly.

"Ok so what do you think is preventing you from being a better you?"

"My past..." I said before telling her the short version of my life story. I told her about the abuse at the hands of my so called mother and stepfather, the betrayal of my friends, and everything else that led up to me being so emotionally fucked up, being sure not to mention their deaths.

"Wow, you have been through a great ordeal," she said shocked.

"You know what's crazy, I read these books and the people just bounce back, that's what I want to be able to do," I said wiping my tears.

"Well this isn't a book or a movie, this is real life and real people don't just bounce back from the kind of abuse you went through."

"I just want to be normal. I want to be able to have the love of my life touch me without me flinching."

"We'll get there, you're session is over."

"That went by fast," I said with a smile.

"Next week will be a little harder, but you can do it," she said with a reassuring smile. When I left her office, I felt good. A little emotionally drained from retelling my story, but overall, I felt a sense of freedom and release. When I got into my car, I looked at my missed calls. Calling Jasmine back first, I waited for her to answer.

"Hey Jas."

"Hey Ma, can you come get me?"

"Where you at?"

"I'm home."

"Uhhhhh I don't know Jasmine."

"Please, I haven't seen you all day."

"Alright, here I come and you better be ready," I said before hanging up. Pulling off, I drove to the house I once shared with my family. Walking up to the front door, I pulled out my keys before remembering that it was no longer my house. I called Jasmine and told her I was outside before turning around to go wait in the car.

"Why not just use your key?" I heard Mega's voice boom from behind me.

"It's not my house anymore so I didn't want to be rude," I said smartly.

"Come on now, Cherish. This will always be your fucking house, I bought it for us."

"I guess, but tell Jasmine I'll be in the car."

"Can we talk?"

"We don't have anything to talk about."

"Man that's bullshit, I fucked up and I know that, but you ain't been telling me about no doctor's appointments, I don't even know what we having cuz you did that on ya own," he said making me feel bad as shit.

"I was so mad at you, but that's no excuse to keep you away from the babies, so for that I'm sorry."

"So what we having?" he asked while rubbing my stomach.

"I don't know, it didn't feel right without you so I told him I didn't want to know," she said with a smile. Kissing my belly, he hugged me tightly. I knew how much these babies meant to him and I would never keep them away from him, I refused to be one of those women.

"You know how much I love y'all?" he asked.

"I know Jason, I know."

"Can we make this work?"

"Honestly, Jason I need to work on my right now, and that's what I'm doing."

"We can work together."

"No, this is something I need to do by myself, and maybe you need time to be sure this is what you want."

"I know you and my babies are what I want," he said grabbing my waist.

"Just please, you're making this harder for me."

"I don't want to do that, but I miss you, shit we miss you," he said referring to Jasmine.

"I see Jasmine every day."

"We miss you here!" he said loudly.

"I will let you be more active, but I'm not coming back yet."

"You still love me lil mama?"

"Always," I said kissing his cheek and getting into my car. When Jasmine got into the car, I pulled off and headed to my new apartment. I just got my furniture delivered and I was happy to be spending my first night here with my baby Jas.

"So this it, do you like it?"

"Yeah, but I wish you were home."

"I know baby, this won't be forever, me and daddy just need some time," I said before showing her her room. After talking for a while, we had a good time watching movies and playing games. I loved this little girl with everything in me and I refused to make her believe that our family was non-existent.

Chapter Sixteen (Mega)

Shit with me and Cherish has been fucked up. She been gone for months and I found out she has her own apartment. We're cordial, she comes to get Jasmine and I've gone to every doctor's appointment involving the twins, and for that, I appreciate her, but shit ain't the same. It's starting to seem like she ain't got no love for a nigga at all no more and that's some shit I can't handle. I ain't never been one of those dudes pressed or stressed over a chick, so this shit right here is new to me. I ain't been fucking with no chicks, thinking bout no chicks, seems like the only woman on my mind is Cherish. Lil mama almost seven months pregnant, shit crazy as hell. Her pregnancy ain't been no walk in the park, but she's handled that shit like a G.

"Good morning Mr. Cruz," Jayda said with a smile. Giving her a simple head nod, I kept it moving. That chick the reason why I ain't got my girl, so all that getting close shit is done. Walking into my office, I started on some paperwork. Things with my record label have been going great, the artist have been rolling in and so has the money. I got a big meeting to sign a new female singer and she's hot as hell and knows it. She has so many offers coming from other labels, but I already know I can take her career to the next level if given the opportunity. This shit is what I'm good at; only thing I can't seem to get right is my own personal shit.

"You have a call on line one," Jayda said through the intercom. Picking up the phone, I was surprised to see it was the school calling.

"Hello Mr. Cruz, I am the school nurse calling about Jasmine."

"Is she ok?"

"Yes, but she got her menstrual cycle in the middle of class. I gave her a change of clothes, but she is very embarrassed and wants to go home."

"Menstrual cycle?" I asked confused. It took a minute for what she was saying to register in my mind and when it did, I was fucked up.

"Wait, you mean her period? She's only nine, naw she can't be, it's too early."

"Sir, these young women are getting it earlier and earlier now a days."

"So what do I do?"

"You come get her, make sure you bring a change of clothes, some Tylenol and just have her mother talk to her."

"Aight, I'm on my way." Grabbing my keys, I headed out while using my phone to call lil mama.

"Everything alright?" she asked with a worried voice when she answered.

"Man hell naw, Jas got her fucking period."

"Oh wow, right now?"

"Yeah, right now. I'm on my way to go get her, but I have this meeting that I can't miss in about forty-five minutes."

"Damn, I'm at my therapy session, call Camille and see if she can watch her for an hour, then I can go get her."

"Aight, imma hit you back, but what do I do about this shit?"

"She had been being a little cranky and I thought it might be coming soon. In our bedroom on my side of the closet there's a gym bag, I got everything she'll need in there. You don't even have to look in the bag, just go get her and give it to her. Tell her I love her and we already talked about this and I will see her in an hour," she said surprising the shit out of me.

"Wait, so you knew this was coming and didn't tell me?"

"I didn't know shit Mega, I'm not fucking psychic, but I did see a few signs."

"Aight Cherish, imma call Camille," I said before hanging up. When I called Camille, she didn't answer, so the only thing I could do is bring her to the office until I figured something out. Picking her up, she looked like a little woman. Although nothing changed physically, she was a little woman in the making, and that scared me. Driving to the house after grabbing Jas, I went exactly where Cherish told me to and sure enough, there was a big ass bag with the word Pink! on it. Grabbing the bag, I took it to Jas.

"You ok?" I asked while we were driving to the office.

"Yeah, me and Cherish talked about this already so I wasn't too surprised, just embarrassed."

"Every female goes through this; you have nothing to be embarrassed about."

"It's this boy in my class and I like him, he's funny and smart and he's always nice to me."

"What about him?"

"Well he was the one who saw my pants, he didn't make fun of me, but I wish I coulda saw it before he did," she said putting her head down.

"First of all, ain't gonna be no liking boys no time soon. Second, shit if I like a woman, I like her no matter what, and a little blood ain't gonna change that," I said with a smile. When we got to the office, I had literally twenty minutes to get to my meeting. Grabbing my phone, I called Camille again and even tried Mama Betty, but no one was answering the phone.

"Hey, who's this beautiful little girl?" Jayda said when we walked into my office.

"Oh Jayda this is Jas, my daughter."

"HI Jas, I'm Jayda, I work with your father."

"I know who you are, and only my friends call me Jas, you can call me Jasmine," she said with an attitude.

"Why you talking to her like that!" I snapped.

"It's cool, I can't be mad that she's over protective about her daddy."

"I'm not over protective, I just don't like you."

"Get in that damn office before I beat ya ass!" I snapped trying to hide my smile. She was reminding me so much of her mother right now it wasn't even funny, and by mother I meant Cherish "Lil Mama" Daniels.

"Don't be so hard on her. It's not her fault, you know Cherish don't like me so who knows what she done told that girl," Jayda said.

"I don't care, that don't make the shit right."

"I know and thank you for defending me."

"No problem," I said before looking at my watch, I had fifteen minutes to get to the meeting and I was really starting to stress the fuck out.

"Is everything ok?" Jayda asked.

"Naw, I got this meeting with Milan and I don't know what to do."

"I'll watch Jasmine," she offered.

"Naw, I don't think that's a good idea."

"Come on, you won't be gone for long," she said with a smile.

"I should be in and out, but let me call my people a few more times," I said before grabbing my phone and calling around.

"Just go, Jason."

"Jas!" I said calling my daughter.

"Yes daddy?"

"I have a meeting to go to but Ms. Jayda is going to watch you until I come back."

"I don't want to stay with her, I don't like her," she said loud as hell.

"Come on now, I promise I won't be long."

"Aight then," she said with a pout.

"That's my baby girl," I said kissing her forehead before heading out to my meeting.

Chapter Seventeen (Jayda)

Shit with me and Mega has been weird as hell ever since the drama went down with Cherish. I just knew if she left him that he would be mine, but all that did was push him further away from me. I offered to watch his disrespectful ass daughter because I wanted to show him that I could be a mother to her. She was a beautiful little girl, and before meeting her, I was excited to become her stepmother, but now that I know what kind of mouth she has, if it were up to me I'd send the little bitch to Dubai as soon as we were married.

"Do you need anything?" I asked Jasmine.

"No," she said rolling her eyes.

"Listen, I don't want you to hate me."

"I don't hate you, I don't know you."

"But you can get to know me, and if you hate me afterwards, I won't bother you again."

"Ok, well I guess I do have a question."

"Ok, ask away."

"What's better for a woman, tampons or pads? I know people my age wear pads, but what if I wanna go swimming," she asked blowing my mind.

"Ummmm I think that's a talk you need to have with your school nurse."

"You told me to ask you anything."

"I know, but I don't want anyone to be mad at me for having a conversation that I shouldn't be having with you."

"Whatever," she said walking away.

"So what do you like to do?" I asked, only to be ignored.

"Do you not hear me talking to you Jas?"

"I asked you not to call me that."

"You know what, imma do some work and you do you."

"Best thing you said since I met you," she said rolling her eyes. I wanted to slap the little bitch, but I knew that she was the only way I could get Mega. If she didn't like me, then I didn't stand a chance with Mega. Walking to my desk, I started in on the paperwork Jason didn't finish. When a half an hour went by, I went to check on Jasmine.

"Hey, you hungry?" I asked.

"No, I'm ok."

"Look, I ain't gonna have you tell ya daddy that I didn't feed you so I need for you to eat."

"I said I'm not hungry, you can't make me."

"When I'm ya new mom I can," I mumbled.

"Who new mom, not mine, I only got one mom and her name is Cherish."

"You a smart mouth lil bitch ain't you," I said through gritted teeth.

"I'm telling my daddy you cussed at me."

"You bet not tell him shit!"

'I'm calling my daddy!" she screamed before standing up to grab the office phone.

"Sit ya little ass down, he's in a meeting, he ain't gonna answer anyways," I said with a smirk.

"Whatever!" she snapped. After making sure her lil grown ass wasn't near the phone, I went to order us some food. She was actually being quiet, she ain't have shit to say to me, but I didn't care as long as she wasn't being a smart ass. When the food came, I offered her some and she turned it down, I could give zero fucks and I hope her ass starved.

"Can I use the bathroom?" she asked.

"I'm sure you know where it's at," I said smartly before continuing to eat my food. When I noticed she still wasn't back from the bathroom, I got up to check on her, only for her to be walking into his office. When I sat back down, I noticed her giving me a look of death. Blowing her a kiss, I laughed my ass off.

"My mama gonna mop the floor with you!" she snapped.

"Let the bitch try it," I said. After I was done eating, I got a call from Mega checking on Jasmine. I watched as Jasmine asked to speak to him, but that wasn't gonna happen, so I ignored her ass and assured Mega that everything was fine.

"Why didn't you let me talk to him!"

"Girl, sit ya ass down!" I snapped back. Before I knew what was happening, Cherish had burst through the office door with a look of anger.

"Jasmine get ya shit!"

"Oh hey Cherish, you here to pick up our daughter," I said laughing.

"You lucky I'm pregnant, with ya thirsty ass!"

"Is you mad or naw?"

"I'm not mad, but you sure will be. You think that Mega would ever look twice at you. Did you really think that if I left him that he would come running to you? Bitch it will never be you, even if I never take him back it will always be me," she said, pissing me off.

"Fuck you!"

"No fuck you bitch, you trying too muthafucking hard and ain't getting nowhere!"

"I swear them niggas should've blown ya fucking brains out!" I slipped up and said.

"Oh yeah, so is that why you mad? You sent them niggas to do something you didn't have the heart to do and they couldn't even do it right," she said laughing hard as hell. I thought she would've been mad or surprised to find out I was the one that tried to get her kidnapped, but her reaction was as if she already knew it was me. I didn't know what to say, and for the first time in a long time, cat had a bitch tongue.

"Oh, you silent now? Yeah Mega might be acting stupid, but I ain't. I don't have a problem with nobody but you bitch, so yeah I knew."

"I'm ready," Jasmine said walking up to us.

"Aight lets go!" she said. When she turned around to leave, Jason was walking in with a confused look on his face.

"Here Jasmine, take the keys and go wait in the car," Cherish said, never taking her eyes off Jason.

"What the fuck is going on!" Mega snapped.

"How dare you leave my fucking child with this bitch, you must have really bumped your fucking head, or is the pussy so good it turned you fucking stupid," she snapped.

"Your child? That ain't even your real daughter!" I screamed. When I said that, Mega tightly grabbed my arm, letting me know to calm my ass down.

"So you gonna let her say that to me mega!" Cherish asked with tears forming in her eyes.

"What happened?" he asked.

"Does it fucking matter, I mean really Jason!"

"I'm trying to understand what the fuck happened Cherish!" Mega said before Cherish reached back and slapped the shit out of him.

"Ask that bitch, cuz I'm done!" she said before storming out.

"I'm so sorry Mega, I was being so nice to your daughter even when she was mean to me," I said with fake tears.

"Why was Cherish so mad?"

"Jason, she doesn't like me and she made your daughter not like me, I don't know what lies she told her."

"Man if it ain't one thing it's another."

"I feel like all this is my fault, I'm so sorry."

"Don't worry about it, but imma head out," he said before leaving. I don't know what the fuck imma do, but more and more I'm losing the man that I love because of this bitch Cherish, and I wasn't feeling it. I've never loved a man the way I love Jason, never met a man quite like him. It's like he's a businessman, but he a thug too. He treats Cherish with so much respect and he is such a good man. When I think about all the men I fucked with wives, fiancés and girlfriends, they didn't think twice about giving up the dick. I need a man that's gonna love me just as much as I love him, and I know Mega is that man.

Chapter Eighteen (Mega)

I don't know what the fuck is going on. I know Cherish doesn't like Jayda, but damn to react that way because of jealousy was petty as hell. I've been calling her for days and she won't answer. I haven't seen my fucking daughter in two days and that shit ain't sitting well with me. I don't know where exactly she lives at and ain't nobody willing to tell me shit. Yeah, maybe I fucked up, but it ain't that serious. I ain't been doing shit but drinking, smoking and fucking stressing. It's one thing to punish me, but don't take my fucking child and not let me see her. Pulling up to Mark's house, I parked and hopped out. I need to talk to my boy since he been through it all with Camille, I knew he would have some kind of solution.

"What's up!" Mark greeted me.

"Man, shit fucked up right now."

"Yeah I heard, you know Cam was the first person she called."

"I ain't seen my daughter in two fucking days."

"Damn that's fucked up."

"Yeah, over some petty shit. She got mad cuz I had Jayda babysit Jas for a fucking hour."

"What's up with you and her?" he asked.

"She feeling a nigga, but I ain't fucking with her like that, it's work and that's it."

"Have you talked to Cherish?"

"Naw, I been calling and she ignoring me, the shit is childish and she showing her age."

"Get the fuck out my house!" Camille screamed.

"Cam, chill the fuck out, don't be kicking my people out!" Mark snapped.

"Fuck both of y'all. I ain't gonna sit here while he bad mouth my fucking friend in my house, y'all can take that shit elsewhere."

"Man you tripping," I said shaking my head.

"I'm tripping, nigga you believed some thirsty ass bitch over ya own fucking child and woman, and I'm tripping, boy bye!"

"I ain't believe nobody over them, I was trying to call and find out what happened and she won't answer."

"It doesn't matter Jason, you being so fucking stupid right now. How did Cherish know that Jas was with that bitch? Obviously something happened, but you were too busy up Jayda's ass to find out the real deal."

"Aight so what happen since you know everything!"

"Oh, fuck you, I ain't telling you shit cuz you don't deserve to know shit. Now either you get out my house or you and Mark asses gotta go!"

"How the fuck you gonna threaten to kick me out my own shit that I pay the bills at, you done lost ya mind!"

"I ain't tryna get you in no shit, so imma head out," I said dapping Mark up and heading out. Picking up my phone, I called Cherish only to be met by her voicemail yet again. She had me on block and that shit was pissing me off. I was missing the shit out of Jasmine and if Cherish was going to continue to play these petty childish games, then I would have to take shit into my own hands. Pulling up to Cherish's school, I parked and walked in to get my baby girl. When she came down to the office she was all smiles until she noticed that it was me who was picking her up, her smile turned into frown.

"Hey baby girl," I said hugging her.

"Daddy, why you picking me up and not Cherish?"

"I missed you, and it's time for you to go home," I said. When she got into the car, it was awkward as hell. She wouldn't talk to me at all and whenever I tried to spark up conversation, she shot that shit down. Pulling up to my house, as soon as I parked, she hopped out the car and slammed my car door. I didn't know what her problem was, but I was ready to beat her ass.

"Jasmine, get your ass down here!" I screamed up the stairs.

"Yes?"

"What the hell is wrong with you?"

"I don't want to be here with you, I want my mom."

"Since when you don't want to be here?"

"Since now, I wanna live with Cherish!" she screamed.

"Lower ya voice Jasmine!"

"Can you please call my mom?" she asked with tears building up in her eyes. To see her so angry with me hurt, especially because I didn't know what I did wrong.

"Why you crying?" I asked before hugging her tightly.

"You believed that girl over me," she said.

"I didn't believe anyone over you, y'all left before I could get y'all side."

"She cussed at me, called me bad names and was mean to me."

"She what!"

"She wouldn't let me call you and she said she gonna be my new mommy. If she is, I want to go live with Cherish."

"She really said those things to you?" I asked only to have her nod her head at me.

"Mommy Cherish was crying because you didn't even try and chase after her, she say you love Jayda."

"How you know all this Jas?"

"I be listening when she talks to Auntie Cam, plus I know when mommy's not happy or she sad."

"Imma make this shit right!" I said before hopping in the car to drop Jas off at Mama Betty's house for a little while. It fucked me up that as soon as I picked her up after not seeing her for days, here I was dropping her off yet again, but I needed to handle this shit right now. Grabbing my phone, I called Jayda and waited for her to answer.

"Hey Jason," she answered.

"Hey, I need to talk to you," I said trying to stay calm.

"Aight, where are you?"

"I'm parked across the street from your building."

"Ok, here I come, but is everything ok?"

"Yeah, just come down," I said before hanging up. When she walked out the building and into my car, I could feel my blood boiling.

"Yo, I just talked to my daughter," I said before pausing.

"Oh, so what, she lied on me again?"

"Stop fucking playing games Jayda, the shit you said to my child is unacceptable!" I snapped.

"I didn't say anything outrageous to your daughter."

"So you weren't cursing at her?"

"Oh God, no!"

"You didn't tell her you were gonna be her new mother?"

"Jason, I love you so much, why can't we be together and raise your daughter?"

"Because she has a mother Jayda, I thought you understood what this was. I don't have those kinds of feelings for you."

"That's a lie. I know you love me, maybe not as much as I love you, but that will change," she said reaching over to kiss me. Pulling my head back, I looked at her, and for the first time since meeting her, I realized that she was a little throwed.

"Jayda, listen to me, I don't love you and never have. I wanted to keep you as an employee, but after all this shit, I gotta let you go," I said.

"Wait, so you firing me?"

"I don't need Jasmine seeing you in the office after what you did to her, and when I get Cherish back, you were gonna have to go anyways, so might as well end this shit now."

"No no no Jason, I need this money!"

"I will write you an awesome recommendation letter and I'm sure you will find a job in no time."

"But me and you are destined Jason."

"Come on now, get out my car!"

"I'm not leaving until you tell me the truth. I know you love me so why are you doing this!" she said as tears poured from her eyes. She had snot dripping down her face; ole girl was a hot fucking crazy mess. Getting out my car, I opened the passenger's side door and tried to pull her out, the crazy bitch had her seatbelt on. Grabbing my gun from my waist, I cocked it back and put it to the side of her head.

"I ain't even bout this life right here, but I need you to get the fuck out my car," I said through gritted teeth. She wasted no time hopping out my shit, but why did I have to threaten to kill her for her to do it, the bitch was crazy. Grabbing my phone, I called Jas to let her know I was on my way, only to have her tell me that Cherish picked her up.

"Yo give ya mama the phone Jas!"

"Ok, hold on."

"Yes, Mega."

"I'm not gonna be playing these fucking games with you, if you done be done, but that's my fucking child and you not gonna keep her from me!" I snapped.

"You're right, I will drop her off at Mama Betty and you do the same. She has a phone so she can call us herself when she's ready to get picked up," she said. I couldn't believe the shit that was coming out her mouth, did we really get to the point where we needed a middle person when it came to handling our child. I was beyond pissed and refused to even entertain the conversation, so instead of saying what I felt, I hung up.

Chapter Nineteen (Cherish)

That nigga got life fucked up if he thought I was gonna just let this shit go, he knew better than to have that bitch watching our child. I don't give a fuck how important that meeting was, nothing is more important than our child and her well-being. The thing that really sent me over the edge was when the bitch said that I wasn't Jayda's real mom, how would she know that unless he told her, and then he didn't even defend me when she said it. I had been keeping Jasmine with me, and not because I was forcing her, but because she didn't want to go with his ass. Numerous times, I tried to take her to him and she would cry. I refused to force that girl to go somewhere she didn't want to go. When I went to pick her up and was told that her father got her early, I wasn't even mad because at the end of the day, that's his child and he loves her so I knew he wouldn't let the shit go for but so long. But when she called me to come get her because he dropped her off at Mama Betty's, to say I was pissed was an understatement. Why the fuck would you go through the trouble of getting her, only to have someone else watch her. When he told Jas to give me the phone, I had the biggest attitude, but when he let me have it, I was actually turned on. Things have been going great with me and it seems like the better I get mentally, the more I miss Jason and what we shared. I had been ignoring him for days and I haven't seen him in weeks, we been doing the drop off plan I suggested and I would be gone before he even got there and vice versa. Today, I had a therapy session and I was dreading it because today I had to role-play and tell everyone that hurt me exactly how I felt. Doc said it was a way to move on and forgive. Walking into her office, the first thing she did when she saw me was give me a pen and paper to write down every person who has been haunting me in my dreams. Giving her the paper, I sat on the couch and prepared myself for this emotional session.

"Ok Cherish, I am Desiree Daniels, your mother, tell me what you want me to know."

"No this is weird," I said.

"Cherish, you ain't shit, never was, never will be which is why I had your stepdad do all those horrible things to you."

"I loved you mommy, even when you hurt me, even when you made me feel worthless, I loved you so much. I thought you were the most beautiful woman in the world and all I wanted was to make you proud. Why couldn't you love me back, why couldn't you be a normal mom? Normal mom's don't burn their children with cigarettes, normal mom's don't try and kill their child, let their man rape their child, normal mom's don't hate their child, I guess I want to know why? Why were these men more important to you than I was, why didn't you feel like I deserved your love!" I screamed. I must have blacked out because when I opened my eyes, I was sitting on the floor in between the doctor's legs while she rubbed my hair and apologized for causing me pain.

"Cherish, now I want you to tell her all that you've accomplished."

"I finished high school a year early, I met the love of my life and I'm pregnant with two beautiful babies. I have friends and family who love me, really love me. I spend Thanksgiving and Christmas with them. It took me a long time to get what I needed and I always thought the love would come from you, that one day you would realize how wrong you were, but that day never came and I'm ok with that because I have people in my life that make up for all the hurt and pain you caused. I guess what I wanna say to everyone that hurt me, my mom, Caesar, Meeka, and Tyree, you guys tried to hurt me, bring me down but none of it worked, I'm still here kicking and swinging and I'm not going out without a fight," I said with a smile as tears flowed down my face.

"How do you feel?" she asked.

"Honestly, I feel like a million pounds have been lifted off my chest," I said. When the session was over, I headed over to Mama Betty's house to pick Jas up. Walking up to the house, I was pissed off to see Mega's ass sitting on the porch as if he were waiting for me to show up.

"Jason, not right now," I said trying to get past him.

"No, we need to talk now!"

"We ain't got shit to talk about!"

"Sit ya stubborn ass down and shut up!" he said. Rolling my eyes at him, I sat down and waited for him to speak his mind.

"I fucked up. I couldn't see how crazy Jayda was and for that, I'm sorry. I didn't want to believe Jayda's side of the story, but you weren't answering my calls, so that was the only side I knew. She no longer works for me, as soon as Jas told me what happened, I brought her here and went to confront and fire Jayda," he said. Now I understood why he just dropped her off.

"So what do you want from me?" I asked.

"I want you, I want my family back, but I know you're working on getting better and I respect that, so for now, I just want my friend back," he said causing me to get teary eyed.

"We can do that," I said with a smile.

"Alright, so set up that appointment so we can find out what we having," he said hugging me. I would be lying if I said being in his arms didn't feel like home. I missed this man so much sometimes my heart hurts, but getting better had to come before all this shit.

"I already set it up for tomorrow, I was actually gonna have Mama Betty tell you to meet me there."

"Aight bet, text me the time and all that good shit and I will be there," he said happily. When we finally left each other, I felt really good. Between my therapy session, and making shit semi right with Mega, I was on cloud nine. Grabbing Jasmine, we went home. I cooked dinner and we had a long talk about me and her father's relationship. I had to let her know that just because I was mad at him, didn't mean she had to be. I appreciated her loyalty to me, but at the end of the day, Jason was an awesome father and she needed to know that. Once Jas was sleep, I called Peter, the realtor I had met. We don't talk everyday because I don't want to give off mixed signals. I already explained to him that I had a lot going on and wasn't really looking for anything, but you know how men can be, so I didn't want to call or text him too much.

"Hey beautiful," he said when he answered.

"Hey Peter, how are you?"

"I'm good, been waiting for you to call me again, I enjoyed our last conversation."

"So did I, but between doctor appointments and everything else, I don't really have time for much else."

"I understand, and trust me I'm not angry, I'm willing to take what I can get."

"Thank you for being so understanding."

"I just wish you would go out with me, on just one date."

"I don't have time for dates, I'm pregnant."

"I don't need all your time, just a few hours. And I already know you're pregnant and I don't care about that."

"Aight, I'll go on one date," I said with a smile.

"Oh snap she said yes!" he said excitedly, causing me to laugh.

"Alright, well I'll text you or call tomorrow so we can plan something," I said before hanging up.

The next morning I was up bright and early to get ready for my appointment, I was excited to know what we were having. I was almost seven months, so this was long overdue. After getting showered, dressed and ready, I dropped Jasmine off at school and headed to my doctor's appointment. When I walked into the office, I was surprised to see that Mega was already there with a big smile on his handsome face.

"Hey lil mama," he greeted me.

"Hey baby daddy," I said laughing.

"Stop playing me with Cherish," he said with a smirk.

"Ms. Daniels," the nurse called.

"Right here," I said walking up to the desk with Mega on my heels.

"The doctor will see you now, you can head on back," she said. Sitting down on the table, I laid back excited and ready.

"I'm so glad you're here Jason."

"So am I," he said grabbing my hand and holding it tight.

"Hello Ms. Daniels, how are you feeling?"

"Hey doc. I feel ok most days, but I'm always tired."

"Yeah, that's what happens when you carry twins, they start to take a toll on your body."

"Well I'm glad it's almost over," I said with a laugh.

"Ok well let's see what we have here," he said lifting my shirt and placing the cold gel on my belly." As he moved the machine around my belly, I was a little nervous at how long it was taking.

"Is everything ok?" Mega asked.

"Oh yeah, here they are. So are you guys ready to find out what you're having?" he said with a smile.

"Hell yeah!" Mega screamed.

"Well Baby A is a beautiful baby…"

"Spit it out!"

"Baby boy," the doctor said laughing. I couldn't hold my tears back, and neither could Jason.

"So I'm having a mini me," Jason said wiping his face.

"Yes, you are. Baby B looks to be a baby girl."

"A girl," I said in disbelief. Don't get me wrong, I was happy to be having healthy babies, but deep down I really didn't want a girl.

"You don't seem excited," the doctor said.

"Can you give us a minute?" Jason asked the doctor.

"Sure," the doctor replied. When he left and closed the door, Mega wasted no time asking me what was wrong.

"I don't know. What if I turn out to be like my mom was?"

"That's never gonna happen, your mom was sick and you're not."

"I know, I'm just scared. I want to be the best mother I can be."

"And you will be, so celebrate this and stop looking at the negatives."

"You're right," I said. Grabbing my phone, I called Camille to tell her the good news and she was excited to be able to start planning my baby shower.

Chapter Twenty (Mega)

Damn, I was having a boy and a girl; I couldn't be happier right now. After helping lil mama clean up the gel off her, she made her next appointment and we headed out. Grabbing her hand, I proceeded to walk her to her car. As we were walking across the street, a car sped up, almost hitting us.

"What the fuck!" I screamed before pushing Cherish out of the way.

"Oh my God, they could have killed us!" Cherish screamed while shaking like a leaf.

"You're ok lil mama, everything's ok."

"You better get that bitch under control!" she said looking at me with evil eyes.

"What you mean?" I asked playing stupid.

"Mega stop acting like you dumb, that bitch is the one that tried to get me kidnapped."

"What, why wouldn't you tell me some shit like that!"

"Because you were so far up that bitch's ass you wouldn't have believed me, just like you didn't believe when I said she keyed my car."

"Man, how you know she did those things though?" I asked.

"I confronted her and she just stood there looking stupid."

"Damn, she on some fatal attraction shit."

"Yeah and you better handle it!"

"Don't worry, I got it," I said before hopping into my car and rushing out of the parking lot. Pulling out my phone, I called Jayda and waited for her to answer.

"Yo, where you at?"

"You fired me so I ended up going back to Atlanta for a little while," she said nervously, confirming that it was her. If she thought I was buying that shit she was crazier than I thought.

"Yeah, aight," I said, hanging up. Instead of leaving like I was going to, I sat outside her apartment waiting to see if she showed up. After waiting for almost an hour, I headed home. I swear that bitch was dead when I got my hands on her. I understand feeling a nigga heavy, but this bitch was on some thin line type shit, and I wasn't feeling it. When I got home, I took a shot of E&J and thought about everything that has happened since meeting lil mama. The fucked up part about it all was that I would do all this shit over again just to be with her and I knew that wasn't going to happen as long as Jayda was around bringing nothing but problems. Grabbing my phone, I called my nigga Mark to see what he was up to.

"Yo, my boy, where you at?" I asked when he answered.

"I'm at the club chilling. Man this wedding shit really starting to fuck with me," he said sounding stressed.

"Yeah this shit with Cherish been getting to me, I'm on my way," I said, hanging up. Grabbing my keys, I drove to the club feeling a little tipsy. Walking into the V.I.P section, I was surprised to see Mark entertaining some bitch.

"Yo, what you doing?"

"I'm cooling."

"Naw bro, I mean why you got this bitch all in ya face?"

"Man, I don't give a shit about this bitch!" he said pushing her off him.

"You love Camille's crazy ass and everybody know it, so don't go fucking it up just cuz you got cold feet."

"It ain't even about the cold feet bro, she don't fucking trust me and that shit getting old," he said taking a shot.

"She don't trust you because of some shit you did, so you can't be mad at her if she need time," I said honestly.

"I fucking love Cam, man. Even though she crazy as shit, I couldn't imagine life without her, but at the same time, I changed my ways for her and still ain't shit changed. When I come home she questioning me like I'm one of the fucking kids.

I'm at this club right now because my business meeting ran late and I'd rather stay here all night than go home and argue with her."

"Damn, so her being insecure is pushing you away like a muthafucka."

"Exactly, and whenever I try and tell her about the shit, she throw in my face that it's my fault that she acts like this. All I can think about is whether or not I want to deal with this shit for the rest of my life."

"Don't give her more fuel to add to the fire. You ain't gotta go home, but don't be sitting in this club. All you need is for her crazy ass to show up here, you already know she gonna shut shit down."

"Yeah you right, imma take my ass home," he said. I was glad when he grabbed his shit and took his drunk ass home. Most niggas didn't know how fucked up it felt to not have a shorty to come home to, but me and Mark knew what that felt like, so I wasn't sure what was on this nigga's brain right now. After having a few drinks by myself, I was about to head out when this bad ass chick walked up to me, smelling like fucking love.

"Why you over here by yourself?" she asked.

"Shit I'm cooling, enjoying a drink," I replied.

"Can I join you?" she said, sitting on my lap. I knew shorty could feel my dick instantly get hard on her ass, it had been way too long since I'd felt the soft ass of a female.

"Naw, I was just about to leave," I said lifting her gently off my lap.

"But you look so sad, you sure you don't need me to make sure you get home safe," she said hitting me with some straight nigga lines that caused me to laugh.

"Naw shawty I'm good," I said getting a good look at her. Shorty had mocha skin that looked soft as hell, a short cut that fit her face real nice and some big ass breasts. She didn't have much ass, but her face made up for what she was lacking in the back.

"So I guess you got a girl at home," she said with a smirk.

"Nope, I ain't got nobody at home but a daughter."

"Damn, so is it me?" she asked pouting.

"Honestly, it ain't you alone, it's all y'all females. I can play this shit out for you. I let you know I ain't looking for a girl, I take you home, fuck you real good with this big dick and after I'm done, I send you on ya way. Now even though I told you what the deal was, you still gonna fall head over heels, either you gonna stalk me, try and kill me or you gonna get me in all kinds of shit with my girl, so naw I ain't taking you home with me, you ain't gotta follow me home. Y'all women are nothing but fucking trouble, and as bad as my dick needs to slide up in something wet and warm, that shit ain't even worth it," I replied with a smirk before throwing the waitress a tip and dipping out. I already had enough shit going on with Jayda and she ain't even get none of this dick, I wasn't gonna add some more bullshit into the mix.

Chapter Twenty-One (Cherish)

The next morning, I met with Camille to shop for some things for the baby shower, but I knew something was up because she asked me to wear all black. When we met up at the mall, she looked sad, but flawless dressed in her all black.

"Are you ok?" I asked.

"Naw I'm not, I think Mark's ass cheating again," she said with a sad and embarrassed face.

"Why would you think that?"

"I can just tell. It's like he isn't really into the whole wedding thing anymore, he's staying out until late and when he is home, it's like he isn't."

"I really don't think he would mess up what y'all have, but I will do whatever you want me to do to help."

"Thanks Cherish," she said hugging me.

"So, you ready to shop?"

"Hell naw, he left early as hell this morning and I'm tracking his phone, we about to follow that ass."

"That's why you said wear black, bitch it's the day time, how we gonna hide?"

"Girl, I don't know. I just always wanted to do some spy shit while wearing all black," she laughed. When we headed out to her car, we followed the GPS to his location and were confused once we got there.

"Bitch, what would he be doing here?" Camille asked me.

"I don't know, shit let's go see," I said before hopping out the car and waddling into the building with Camille behind me. Walking into the dance studio, we watched as Mark slow dance with some old ass lady. Once again, Camille's ass was standing there looking stupid. Grabbing her arm, we slowly backed out of the studio without being seen.

"Bitch, you sent us on a dummy mission," I said laughing.

"How was I supposed to know this nigga was taking dancing classes?" she said laughing.

"Girl, you need to learn how to trust that man because he loves you."

"So what about him staying out all late and shit?"

"I don't know, but I say ask him instead of playing inspector gadget."

"Whatever, you ready to go shopping?"

"I been ready!" I said hyped. We ran through the mall shopping for things for the baby as well as things for my baby shower. Camille's wedding was in less than a month so she had everything already together for that.

"So I wanted to know if you would be a bridesmaid?" she asked once we sat down.

"Shit, I thought I was already gonna be one," I pouted.

"You were, but I still needed to ask so fix ya face cry baby."

"Uh huh."

"So what you doing after you leave here?" she asked.

"Shit, Mama Betty has Jasmine and your kids so I decided to take the handsome realtor up on his offer."

"Yasssss bitch, you young and you deserve to be taken on a nice date boo."

"You don't think it's a bad thing?"

"No, I don't. Girl go have fun and stop thinking so much."

"Thank you," I said hugging her.

"Oh shit I forgot. Are you coming to my wedding rehearsal tomorrow night?"

"Yeah, you know I wouldn't miss it."

"I'm just asking because Mega's gonna be there. Girl I tried to tell Mark that he was no longer in my wedding and he went the fuck off."

"You a mess, I don't care if that man is around, we've actually been getting along, aside from the fact that he still hasn't found that crazy bitch Jayda," I said, shaking my head.

"Fuck that bitch, she ain't crazier than me, and I put that on my life. I will shoot first and ask questions later if I catch her thirsty ass tryna run my fucking friend over and shit!" Camille said, getting hyped as hell. The day it happened, I had to beg her not to go looking for Jayda's dumb ass. Camille's wedding and my baby shower were so close and we didn't need her in jail.

"Don't worry, she ain't gonna stay hidden. When I have my baby imma beat that bitch ass like she stole something."

"Girl bye, you see how broad that bitch shoulders are, we gon have to tag team that ho," Camille said, causing me to laugh. After talking for a while, me and Camille went our separate ways. After leaving Camille, I got a text message from Peter telling me to meet him at a park. The next message he sent was the address. I would be lying if I said I was excited, I thought he would take me to some fancy restaurant, but instead, I'm meeting him at a park. Hopping in my car, I drove to the address he sent and was taken aback by how huge and beautiful this park was. I had every intention of taking Jas and the twins here in the future. Looking around, I spotted him by the swings. Walking over to him, he gave me a friendly hug. Taking my hand, he led me to the swing. I was a little nervous. First off, I was pregnant and second I hadn't been on a swing since before my grandmother died. Sitting on the swing, he pushed me lightly.

"So, tell me about yourself?"I asked as he pushed me on the swing.

"Well my name is Peter, I'm a realtor, but you already know all that, I'm twenty-five, no children and I love life."

"Do you want children?" I asked.

"Of course I do, one day and with the right woman."

"So what made you ask me out?"

"I thought you were beautiful, I loved your chocolate skin that seemed to glow, your smile and you had a kind, welcoming soul that was hard to miss," he said, causing me to smile hard.

"Thank you!" I said. We continued to talk for over an hour after, swinging on the swings. We sat on a bench in the park until my ass started to hurt. I didn't really want to end the day because I had so much fun and he was such a nice person.

"Well this was fun and hopefully we can do it again," he said kissing my cheek before helping me into my car. When I pulled off, I felt good, but walking into my apartment, it was quiet and I was feeling lonely and bored as hell after a while. I made dinner, which consisted of fried pork chops, baked mac and cheese balls, and a chef salad with extra Italian dressing.

After eating, I tried to find a movie to watch on demand and like always, there was nothing on. Grabbing my phone, I called the only person who I knew would answer and prayed that he wasn't busy.

"Yo, you aight!"

"Yeah I'm good, calm down," I said laughing.

"Oh, well I ain't use to you calling."

"Yeah I know, but I was calling because I made dinner and wanted to know if you wanted to come over."

"Oh shit you giving me the address," he said laughing.

"Shut up, either you want to come or not."

"Yeah I'll be there, just send the address," he said.

"Aight, imma text you," I said before hanging up. After sending him the address, I poured me a medium sized glass of red wine to relax, turned on some music and waited. A half an hour later, I jumped up after hearing a knock at the door. I wasn't sure why I was so nervous, but this shit was making me mad as hell. Opening the door, I stood in front of him with his old basketball shorts on, a sports bra and my hair tied in a scarf.

"Damn, you look beautiful," he said, causing me to laugh.

"Boy shut up," I said nervously. Moving me to the side, he walked into my apartment and walked around my shit like he owned it before nodding his head in approval.

"This shit aight," he said with a smirk.

"Well it's all I need for me and my little family."

"Oh, so what you think imma let you raise my kids in a fucking two bedroom condo," he said in disbelief.

"You can't let me do shit, but yeah imma raise them here," I said lying.

"Yeah aight, so what you make?" he said changing the subject. After disappearing into the kitchen, I came out with a huge plate of food for him and a cup of apple-cranberry juice, his favorite. We both sat in the living room, eating silently. It's crazy that I could be so nervous around the only man that I've ever loved.

"So how you been?" I asked.

"Same shit, gettin this money and tryna get you back," he replied.

"Ummmm you wanna watch a movie?" I asked.

"Yeah, what you got?"

"I got *The Perfect Guy*," I said. After putting the movie in, we both got comfortable on the couch. This movie was actually good as shit, but I was so tired sleep took over and before I knew it, I was knocked out. When I woke up and looked at the time, it was ten o'clock in the morning. I ain't slept that long since leaving the home I shared with Mega. Looking around, I was surprised that he had left without so much as a goodbye. Getting up, I hopped in the shower and the only thing I could think about was Mega and how much he made me feel at peace and loved. Damn, I was missing that man something crazy and all I wanted to know was if he was missing me as much as I was missing him. After my shower, I got dressed and went to meet Camille at the venue where she was having her rehearsal dinner. I knew she was gonna be mad because I was supposed to have been here early to help her set up. She was such a bridezilla that she ended up firing everyone she hired and the last chick she actually cursed her out and they almost got into a fist fight. I understand her wanting everything perfect, but like I told her, the only way to get shit exactly how you want it is to do it yourself. Walking into the venue, I was taken aback, it was so beautiful and I knew this was exactly what Camille wanted, so I was happy. Pulling out my phone, I called Camille to see where she was. Looking up, I saw her arguing with Mark. I wanted to walk away, but Mark looked as though he needed saving.

"Yo, you been acting fucking crazy since I proposed. If you don't trust me, then don't marry me!"

"Maybe I won't!"

"What the hell is going on?" I asked.

"Talk to your friend!" Mark said before walking away.

"What happened?" I asked Camille who was on the verge of tears.

"Everything is all bad," she said before breaking down. I felt so bad for her. Every movie or show I've seen, the bride was happy, and knowing that my friend wasn't happy hurt me.

"Why is it all bad Cam?" I asked hugging her.

"I didn't want to tell Mark, but my mom ain't coming," she said.

"You need your mom there. Why isn't she coming?"

"Man, my mom doesn't think Mark is good enough, and she never did. We got into it heavy when she found out I was pregnant and she supposedly had a change of heart and I thought everything was good, but when I told her we were getting married, she went the fuck off."

"Wow, that's fucked up, she is supposed to be there to support you."

"I love Mark with all my heart and I've always been team fuck the haters, but now it's weighing heavy on me."

"Why haven't you just told Mark about what's going on instead of pushing him away?"

"Because I know he gonna say fuck her, we don't need her there, but I need her there Cherish, I really do," she said. As I held her, my heart really broke for her. I didn't have family that could disapprove of my marriage, so I couldn't imagine how she was feeling right now.

"I say tell him exactly how you feel Camille, you don't always have to be this strong person, everyone needs their mother sometimes."

"Thanks boo. My dad is coming though, and besides the money he's sent me we haven't really communicated much, he hasn't even seen Mylee."

"Why?"

"It's my fault. I love my mom so much that when he left I hated him for hurting her, I hated him for her and never gave him a chance."

"So does she know your father will be there?"

"No, but I really don't care. They haven't been together for years; I just want her to move on."

"I understand, you know I got you're back, but ain't nothing like having the back of your husband, so tell him so that he can be there to support you."

"I swear imma tell him what's going on with me. I feel so bad taking my anger and stress out on him, I know he ain't cheating, but blaming my problems on him is easier than dealing with the real problem.

"Oh, you know I know all about that," I said laughing.

"Yeah, Mega done pissed me off, but I know he loves you and he's a good guy."

"Well today ain't about him, it's about you and this rehearsal dinner, so come on so we can finish setting up," I said with a smirk. After we got done fixing up the venue, the people started pouring in and I was getting more and more excited for Camille. This dinner made the fact that she was getting married soon seem all too real.

"Come here Cherish!" Camille called out to me. Walking over to her, she was standing with an older handsome man and a woman in her late thirties.

"Hey boo."

"I wanted to formally introduce you to my dad, Raphael," she said with a smile.

"It's so nice to meet you!"

"Nice to meet you as well. Camilla has told me nothing but good things about you."

"Camilla?" I asked, looking at Camille.

"Wow, my name is Camille daddy!" she said before trying to storm away.

"Don't tell me what your name is, I named you myself!" he said proudly.

"But my name is Camille daddy."

"Your mother changed your name to spite me. I named you Camilla, after your big sister that passed away," he said sadly.

"Big sister?"

"Yes, your mother never told you about your older sister?" he asked.

"No, I thought I was an only child."

"You had an older sister that died of SIDS when she was an infant. Your mother took her death extremely hard and instead of embracing her short life and sudden death, she wanted to pretend as if she never existed."

"I can't believe she would do that!"

"Don't be angry with your mother Camilla, I know she probably smothers you, but she can't handle losing another child in any way."

"I understand, but damn, not telling me was selfish as hell."

"Ummmm I'll let y'all talk, would you like to come to the buffet with me?" I asked her father's wife.

"I would love to," she said walking away with me.

"Thank you for taking me with you, even though they were aware of me standing there, I felt like I was eavesdropping," she said with a laugh.

"So did I and it's no problem," I said smiling.

"How many months are you?" she asked.

"Oh I'm seven months," I said proudly rubbing my belly.

"With twins huh?"

"Yeah, how did you know?"

"I'm a gynecologist; I can tell by the way you're carrying."

"I read that somewhere, but I thought it was a myth."

"Oh, no it's not, I mean I wouldn't use this method to tell a mother what she's having, but I do it in my head," she said laughing.

"I wanted to become a doctor at one point."

"Why not do it, you seem like a bright young lady."

"With twins coming and how difficult medical school can be, I don't think I can do it."

"You can do anything you put your mind to."

"Thank you," I said with a smile. She seemed really kind hearted and sweet, just from this conversation alone, I could see why Camille's father married her. We continued to talk while Camille and her father caught up. I was enjoying her company until I felt someone behind me. When I looked up, I was staring face to face with the love of my life.

"What's up lil mama," he said kissing my cheek.

"Hey Mega," I said nonchalantly.

"Why you being like that?"

"The same reason you left my apartment early as hell without saying anything!" I snapped without meaning to.

"Woah, why you got an attitude? I didn't think you wanted me there and I didn't mean to fall asleep, so I left when I woke up."

"Whatever," I said before turning my focus back onto Samantha.

"I'm sorry about that, that's my children's father and he irks my entire soul."

"That's how every woman is during a pregnancy," she said laughing.

"Hmmmm mmmmm I don't know about that."

Chapter Twenty-Two (Mega)

I knew Cherish would be upset, but I wasn't gonna keep playing these games with her, shit she lucky I came over last night. One minute she hates my guts and I can't get so much as a text back, then in the same breath, she's calling me asking me to come over for dinner. If she doesn't want to be with me then I can't keep doing the back and forth shit, it ain't good for me or Jasmine. When she fell asleep last night her phone went off, I opened the text only to find out that she went on a date earlier that day, but calling me over later that night get the fuck outta here.

"What up?" I said, dapping Mark, Kasan, Chris and Terrence.

"Shit, these niggas over here stressing over these crazy chicks," Kasan said laughing.

"Nigga shut ya ass up, I know you be at home crying, wondering when Shante gonna come back!" Mark said laughing.

"Fuck you!"

"Y'all funny as hell," I said, shaking my head.

"So I heard Cherish lil cute ass kicked you to the curb," Kasan said laughing.

"Fuck you nigga, imma get lil mama back!" I said fake fighting Kasan.

"Man on some real shit though, I don't know what's going on with Camille, she been snapping on a nigga on a regular basis."

"Shorty just stressed about the wedding," Chris said.

"Yeah, you might be right," Mark replied.

"Real talk nigga, you gonna have to pull out all the stops to win lil mama back," Mark said seriously.

"I know, but I'm trying to wait until after she drops my babies," I said before showing them the ultrasound pictures on my phone.

"Damn, you bout to be a dad to not one baby, but two," Kasan said.

"Yeah, I got my baby girl Jas, and now imma have two more, but I'm happy as hell," I said happily.

"Y'all niggas raise y'all glasses. My nigga done did the unthinkable, he marrying the love of his life, and real talk I'm the older cousin, but I look up to this nigga for stepping up and making shit right with crazy ass Camille, y'all fit each other like a fucking puzzle piece. Congrats!" Kasan said before we took the shots back.

"Thanks, all y'all got the perfect women. Chris, Queesha love ya dirty draws my nigga. Terrence we ain't known you long, but you came at the perfect time because Shana has been hurt badly. Kasan, my nigga you fucked up royally, but we all know how much you love Shante's stubborn ass, you just make sure when you get her back you treat her right. And my nigga Mega, you got you a real keeper. This chick done been through hell, literally, and without you who knows where she would be right now. You ain't really fuck up in my opinion, but you hurt an already hurt girl, so you have some making up to do. Over all like I said, we got some good ass females in our lives and don't let me be the only one to make an honest woman out of one of them."

"Yo, you soft as shit!" Kasan screamed.

"Aight, don't say I didn't try and school y'all dumb ass negroes," he said shaking his head "Nigga don't say we didn't try and warn you, Camille crazy as hell," Kasan said laughing.

"Hell yeah she is, she done corrupted my lil mama!" I cosigned.

"I already know my wife crazy and I love it, she be ready to bust her gun for a nigga."

"True, ain't nothing wrong with a down ass crazy chick," Terrence said with a laugh.

"Fellas I'll be back, imma go mess with my future," I said before walking away from them. I watched as lil mama talked to the lady and I couldn't help but notice how beautiful she looked carrying my babies inside of her. She had the brightest glow, and although this pregnancy has been hard on her, you wouldn't be able to tell. She was wearing a long flowing red maxi dress with a little sweater over it and instead of wearing heels; she had on a pair of red and white Adidas. I thought she looked so sexy. I was use to women wearing high heels and short dresses, but looking at Cherish was like a breath of fresh air. Her chocolate skin was glistening and she didn't have on a bit of makeup, she was simple and I loved that about her.

"Can I talk to you for a minute?" I asked, standing behind her.

"I'm keeping Samantha company, Jason," she replied.

"I'm ok, go head and talk to this handsome man," the woman said with a smile. Helping Cherish out of her chair, we walked over to a more quiet area.

"You know I miss you, right?" I asked her.

"I miss you too Mega," she said nervously.

"Why can't we try and work this out?"

"I already told you why, I just need to deal with things alone."

"But you're not alone!"

"See, why you gotta start being loud?" she said attempting to get up and walk away.

"I'm sorry, don't leave. This shit is just stressful, I need you with me."

"I can't do that right now. I can't love you or our kids until I learn to love and accept myself."

"So you want a nigga to wait around for you?" I said out of anger and confusion.

"Wow, no I do not want a *nigga* to wait around for me, I never asked you to."

"So you good not being with me?"

"I never said that!"

"You didn't have to say shit, you're actions said it all. You left me because you needed some space so you say, but you going on dates and shit

"I didn't do shit but go to the park with him damn. Did you forget about you and that bitch Jayda and what ya ass did. Fuck all that why are you even going through my phone!"

"Do you blame me for getting close with her as much as you push me away? I didn't do shit but love and support you all for you to push me away cuz what that pervert nigga did to you. You don't want to admit it cuz it's so easy for you to blame me for everything, but you're the reason why we're fucked up!" I snapped.

"You know what Jason, this conversation needs to take place at another time," she said getting out the chair and waddling away. I swear I played this conversation out totally different in my head. I thought I would pour my heart out to her and she would see how much I love and miss her and come running home. Instead, I let my anger get the best of me. I mean what the fuck, I'm a good ass nigga, I don't and shouldn't have to wait around for her.

"You know what Cherish; you go head and do you, cuz I plan on doing my own thing. Fuck is you to think imma wait around for you to snap your fingers and take me back!" I screamed. Stopping in her tracks, she turned around and looked at me through teary eyes before turning around and walking away.

"Really Mega, did you have to embarrass her like that!" Camille screamed.

"Man fuck her, she wanna act like I cheated or some shit!"

"This is my rehearsal dinner; you should have waited to talk about that shit!"

"Waited until when? It's like pulling teeth to get as much as a text back from her ass."

"You are so fucking selfish," Camille said shaking her head and walking away to catch lil mama.

"Nigga you tipsy as hell, you need to go home and sleep this shit off," Chris said.

"Imma little fucked up, but everything I said I fucking meant. She wanna be done, she wanna play games, fuck her!"

"You don't mean that nigga," Mark said shaking his head.

"Man fuck this, I'm out!" I said before leaving. When I got home, I took my ass to sleep and that shit felt good as hell. Ever since Cherish left, I ain't been doing shit but stressing about her ass, well all that shit is done.

Chapter Twenty-Three (Cherish)

"I can't believe Jason said those things to me, but what hurt the most was that he was right," I said to my therapist.

"So you admit that it's your fault?"

"I'm not saying it's all my fault because he shouldn't have been entertaining that bitch, but maybe I kind of pushed him away and into the arms of her. I just wasn't over the things that happened in my past," I said honestly.

"Don't you think that you guys should talk about this?" she asked.

"I don't have anything to say to him right now. You told me not to react off of anger, and if I spoke to him, that's exactly what would happen."

"What are you so angry with him about?"

"He embarrassed me at that dinner."

"No Cherish, you were mad at him before that. Even though you knew he didn't sleep with that girl, you still reacted as though he did, which is understandable to a certain extent, but even after time passed, you still haven't forgiven him. So my question is why are you so upset with him?"

"I don't know."

"You do know, maybe you're not ready to let it out."

"So what should I do?" I asked.

"I can't tell you what you should do Cherish. This is your life and every decision in it should be up to you, but what I will say is talking about it makes it easier to handle, so maybe it is best if you set up a group session."

"Maybe you're right, I'll think about it."

"Alright, so aside from you relationship issues, how else has your past been affecting your present?"

"I have been really good, and for the most part, happy. The only thing now is the fact that I'm having a daughter and that scares the shit out of me. I mean, I am my mother's daughter so what if I turn out just like her. I couldn't imagine doing the things my mother did to me to my own children, but it still scares me."

"What exactly makes you think that you will turn out like her, you are her child, but you aren't her, you're Cherish and you are a good person."

"My friend Camille said the same thing," I said laughing through my tears.

"Well you should listen to her, she sounds like a smart girl," she said with a laugh. We continued to talk for another hour. I swear making the decision to see a therapist was the greatest thing I could have ever done. She has helped me more in these few weeks than I would have ever imagined. When the session was over, I called Peter and explained to him that as much as I enjoyed his time and being in his space, I couldn't see him again for personal reasons. Now just wasn't a good time for me. I thought he would get upset, but instead, he was understanding and told me to call him when I was ready. After hanging up with him, I rushed to get Jasmine from Mama Betty's house; she had been keeping her a lot of days. She said Jasmine had an old soul and was a good helper; it gave both me and Mega a lot of free time. Parking my car, I walked up to Mama Betty's only to be met by Mega. I was having a good damn day so far and didn't need him ruining it.

"I wasn't sure how long your session was gonna last so I came over to spend some time with her until you came," he said before hugging Jasmine and walking away to his car. Was it weird that although I said I didn't want to deal with his shit, I was highly upset that he didn't try to say anything to me. I mean what the fuck, how he gonna snap on me for going on a date? I do what I think is the right thing and end something that didn't even get started for the sake of my relationship with Mega's ass, only to have him basically ignore me.

"Ummmm ok, well how are you?" I said as he walked away.

"I'm good, how are you and my babies?" he asked.

"Their good, kicking up a storm," I said with a laugh.

"Aight, well let me know when the next appointment is," he said before getting into his car and pulling off, leaving me standing there with my mouth open. Instead of going home like I intended on doing, I drove to Camille's house to vent.

"So let me get this straight, you told him you needed time for you, and because he decided to give you that, you're feeling some type of way?" Camille said looking confused.

"Stop acting like I'm crazy bitch. I know I said I needed time, but I didn't think he would accept that," I pouted.

"He didn't accept it. He fought you tooth and nail; hell got drunk and acted a fool at my dinner."

"I know but…"

"Ain't no but's bitch, you said you needed time, and he giving you that."

"Shut up, you're the one that agreed that I should leave."

"No, I told you I would have your back no matter what you chose, you said you needed to work on you and I agreed with that," she corrected.

"I guess."

"Aight, now let's talk about this baby shower. I got games, food, prizes and everything," she said excitedly.

"Well I'm ready for these damn babies to come," I said rubbing my belly.

"I felt the same way and I was only carrying one. Girl, I couldn't be you right now."

"Gee thanks."

"You know what I mean, you handling it well. I mean shit, you look good."

"I pee every second, I'm emotional as hell, I'm always farting and I eat the weirdest shit, but you right, at least I look good," I laughed.

"So I told Mark about my mama and he actually felt bad for me and offered to talk to her," she said happily.

"See, I told you he would be there to support you."

"Yeah plus my father told me some shit I really wasn't expecting."

"So what are you gonna do about that?"

"I wanted to have a dinner, but I'm so damn nervous."

"Oh you don't think people gonna like you're food?" I asked.

"Uh huh bitch you tried it, this ain't got shit to do with my food, I just don't know whether or not I should invite my dad," she said rolling her eyes.

"Oh ok, I mean if you do invite him tell his ass to leave the wife at home. I like her a lot and I would hate to have to go to her funeral cuz ya mama killed her ass," I said laughing.

"Trust me I know that already, but foreal, you don't like my food?"

"Yeah, I like it," I lied.

"Oh ok, well fuck everybody who don't cuz my bestie Shante loves it too," she said proudly. I couldn't do shit but shake my head. I haven't met Shante yet, but I knew both of us were going to hell for lying to that girl.

"Well I gotta start my dinner so imma head out," I said hugging her.

"Aight boo," she said. When I got home, I couldn't help but think about Mega and all the ways he had me fucked up. I knew he loved me so these little games he playing by acting like he could care less wasn't gonna work. Yeah, I was talking a good game, but everybody and they mama knew what Mega was doing was working like a muthafucka, but I wasn't gonna tell him that.

Chapter Twenty-Four (Cherish)

Today was the day of Camille's little dinner she put together so that her parents could talk and hash out any differences they were having before her wedding. She asked me to come and show my support and of course, I showed up with bells on.

"Hey boo, thank you for coming. It's just gonna be you, me, Mark and my parents."

"That's fine; I know you need all the support you can get," I said laughing.

"You damn right, cuz when my mom comes and finds out my dad is here, she gonna flip the fuck out, she doesn't even know that I'm in contact with him like that."

"Wait, you didn't tell her?"

"No, but now that I got you here, imma tell her tonight," she said smiling.

"See bitch you wrong for that," I said shaking my head. I never even met her mom before, now imma be known as the chick that witnessed all the drama. Camille had a whole set up on the table, and as soon as I stuck my hand in the potato salad, I knew that she didn't make it. I couldn't help but think that maybe tonight was gonna go better than I suspected. The first person to arrive was Camille's father. I liked him; he was very sweet and gave off a father vibe that I'd never got the pleasure of feeling.

"It's nice to see you again," Camille's father said hugging me.

"Same here," I replied with a smile.

"Ok daddy, mommy just called and she's on her way, please be nice and hear her out."

"I'm always nice, it's her that's the devil," he said nastily.

"Cherish, please sit next to him and make sure he behaves, me and Mark will sit next to my mom," she whispered to me. Damn, she was making seating arrangements and all; I was starting to get worried. Within twenty minutes, the doorbell rang and I could literally see the fear and nervousness in Camille's face, and I was nervous for her. Getting up, Camille went to open the door, and the look on her mother's face when she saw Camille's father sitting next to me, was priceless.

"Oh hell no Camille, have you lost your damn mind!" she snapped.

"Don't you mean, Camilla?" she said rolling her eyes.

"You told her!" she screamed, looking at Camille's father.

"You left me no choice, why didn't you tell her about our daughter!" her father's voice boomed.

"Fuck you, I'm surprised you don't have that home wrecking bitch here with you!"

"Ma, don't talk about Samantha that way, she is really nice."

"Oh, you bet not say shit to me Camille. Why the fuck would you contact this nigga? Besides money, what has he ever done for you!"

"He is my father. Damn, all this shit is stressing me out, I need both of y'all at my wedding."

"Oh, if you thought me finding out you were marrying that hoodlum was bad, this shit is even worse."

"You don't like me, I get it, but what you not gonna do is disrespect me in my home. Hoodlum or not, your daughter loves me!" Mark snapped.

"Listen, maybe y'all should just sit down and take a breather," I said calmly.

"Who the hell are you? Don't tell me you're this nigga's child, little girl mind ya business!" she said, shutting my ass up.

"Don't talk to her like that and don't talk about my fiancé like that. Whether you come or you don't, that's something you have to live with, but either way I'm marrying this man and my father is walking me down the aisle."

"You so fucking ungrateful, Camille," her mother said shaking her head.

"I thought we could work this out, but obviously we can't," Camille said as tears fell from her eyes. Looking into her mother's stubborn face, Camille shook her head and walked away, we didn't even get a chance to eat, shit went downhill fast.

"Listen, you don't know me, but I'm good friends with Camille and all she wants is your love and support. This is supposed to be the best time in her life, and because of all of this. It's the worse. If you love your daughter like I know you do, then you would put the drama aside and be there for her," I said walking away. Going upstairs, I went to check on Camille, and what I saw broke my heart. She was lying in bed balling her eyes out in the fetal position. Sitting on her bed, I held her tight, hugging her.

"It's ok boo," I said.

"I just wanted everything to be perfect, and this is far from it."

"I understand, but at the end of the day, the only person by your side is your man. Him, Mylee and Sparkle, they're your new family," I said honestly.

"You're right, but I just thought I would have my mom helping me get ready on my wedding day."

"I can imagine how bad that hurts, shit I won't have my mom at my wedding either. Even if she was alive, I doubt she would have been there. Yeah that hurts, but I know Mega got my back, no matter what."

"You're right, this hurts, but I will get over it I guess."

"You aight babe?" Mark asked, walking into the room.

"Yeah, I'm good."

"I'm sorry this shit ain't work out the way you wanted it to," he said, kissing her.

"Well you're in good hands so imma head out," I said smiling at the love her and Mark shared.

"Aight boo, thank you for coming," she said before I walked out. When I got home, once again I was alone. Times like this made me really miss Jason a lot. Grabbing my phone, I shot him a text.

Me: Wyd

Mega: I'm out…

Me: Do you want to come over?

Mega: Are the babies ok?

Me: Yeah

Mega: Well naw I'm good…

Me: Seriously, what are you doing that's so important or should I say who?

Mega: Think what you want, if I was doing somebody you can't be mad, you done with me, remember...

Me: Fuck you Jason

I had to have read those messages at least ten times before tossing my phone on my bed. He had to have been fucking with somebody; why else would he be acting brand new like this. Lying back in bed, I let sleep take over my body.

Chapter Twenty-Five (Mega)

Sitting at the bar, I took shot after shot. Cherish doesn't know how hard turning her down was for me. Lil mama the love of my life, but I can't continue to play these games with her. I can't continue to let her string me along whenever she fucking felt like it. Truth is, she had me stressed the fuck out, I ain't never drank so much in my life, I'm slacking as far as work, this ain't even like me.

"You ok?" someone asked.

"Yeah, I'm good," I said without looking up at the girl with the pretty voice.

"You don't seem good, but aight then cry baby," she said, causing me to snap my head up. Staring at her, I was trying to place her face.

"What you say?"

"I said you a cry baby, this the second time I done seen you sitting by ya self all sad."

"Don't I know you from somewhere?" I asked

"Yeah, I'm Kaliah, we met a while back and you were sad then too."

"I ain't sad, just got a lot of shit on my mind," I said. getting defensive.

"Well like I offered last time, let's go back to my place and I can show you an awesome time," she said with a confident smirk.

"You know what, fuck it," I said taking back my last shot and getting up.

"Follow behind me," she said hopping into her car. As I followed her to Camden, I couldn't help but think what the fuck am I doing right now. Pulling into a parking spot beside her, I watched as she hopped out the car looking just as beautiful as she did when I first met her.

"Damn, you shoulda told me you lived in the projects."

"Oh, what you scared nigga?" she asked with a smirk.

"I ain't never scared, but I definitely wouldn't have left the burner," I said laughing. Following her into her apartment, the inside looked totally different from the outside. She had a nice little town house that was nicely decorated.

"You coming?" she asked as she walked to the back room. I mean damn she didn't wanna talk, get to know each other, nothing, I swear this shit with Cherish had me feeling like a little bitch. Following her to the back, I walked into the room and couldn't help the laugh that left my mouth, what the fuck was this.

"Yo, you gotta be kidding me!" I said in disbelief.

"I told you I would make you feel good, now sit the fuck down so I can beat that ass," she said, tossing me a PS4 remote. She had her back room set up like a mini arcade; she had a pool table and the whole nine. Sitting down, we got straight to business and I was actually feeling a lot better.

"So what's up with you and ole girl?"

"Man she pregnant with my babies, but she's been through a lot, and although I ain't the best nigga, she taking shit out on me that I don't deserve."

"I heard pregnant chick hormones be crazy."

"Yeah, but what's up with you? Ya ass went from trying to bag a nigga to this," I said laughing.

"I was looking to take something home and fuck, I didn't see you as nothing but that, but then I saw ya face and you gave me that crazy ass speech I was like this nigga in love," she said with a laugh.

"Damn you was gonna use me?"

"Y'all do the shit all the time, so miss me with the BS."

"You right," I said, still whooping her ass in Mortal Combat. We took shots, played games and she wasn't bad to look at, and the best part of all of this was she didn't want my ass. By the time I checked my phone, it was four-thirty am.

"Damn, I gotta get outta here," I said putting the controllers down.

"Aight, well I'm glad I could make you feel better," she said with a smile.

"Yeah you did that, next time it's on me."

"Aight bet, well you got my number nigga, just hit me up," she said before walking into a room I'm assuming is her bedroom.

"And lock the door!" she screamed. When I got outside, I checked my call log and text messages, and sure enough, there were four from Cherish cursing me out, asking me where I'm at and what I'm doing. Pulling up to my house, I unlocked the door and stepped inside, tired as hell. Turning on the light, I was surprised to see Cherish.

"Yo, what you doing here?" I asked, but on the inside, I was laughing my ass off.

"What you mean what I'm doing here? Last I checked you bought this house for me too," she said with an attitude.

"Cherish, cut the shit, you know you don't live here no more so what's up?"

"It's five in the morning, where were you?"

"You tripping."

"So it's ok for me to stay out till five?" she asked.

"I mean, you are almost eight months pregnant and all, but sure, you can do what you want when you're single," I said with a smirk.

"So were you with Jayda?"

"Hell naw, fuck that bitch!" I said, meaning every word.

"You know what, fuck you, I'm out!"

"Stop being dramatic lil mama, it's five am just sleep in the guest bedroom."

"No, imma sleep in my bed."

"Ok, well I'll sleep in the guest room," I said, refusing to give her the argument she wanted.

"I can't stand you!"

"I know; I'm assuming that's why you ended things with me," I said walking away. When I got upstairs, I noticed a text message from Kaliah.

K-Dawg: You in safe?

Me: Yeah why the hell would you program that shit as ya name?

K-Dawg: Didn't want ya wife gettin suspicious.

Me: I'm single…

K-Dawg: Well in that case you can call me whateva ya likeeeee lol I'm tired ttyt.

"Who got you smiling?" Cherish asked, walking into my bedroom.

"Nobody..." I said putting my phone down.

"Yeah, whatever."

"What is wrong with you?"

"Nothing..."

"Something wrong so go head and speak up."

"I said nothing!" she snapped before rushing out. The next morning, I woke up and she was gone. I wasn't trying to hurt lil mama, I just needed her to understand she can't keep playing fucking mind games and stringing me along.

"Hey, daddy!"

"Hey, baby girl."

"I made you breakfast," she said, causing me to smile.

"You did, I must be the luckiest daddy in the world."

"Yeah you are; I don't just cook for any daddy, only you."

"You are something else," I said getting up. When I got downstairs, breakfast was laid out and I instantly knew who had cooked it.

"Lil mama cooked this before she left?" I asked before digging in. I haven't had her food in weeks.

"Yeah, she told me to wake you up after she left."

"Aight thanks, with ya lyin ass."

"I didn't lie, I cracked the eggs."

"Oh shit, my baby a cook now," I said kissing her cheek. After eating and cleaning up the kitchen, I went to go get showered and dressed. I was spending the entire day with my beautiful baby girl.

"Can we go to the mall?"

"Anything you want."

"Can mommy come?"

"Anything you want, I'm not sure if she will, but you can try."

"Thanks daddy!" she said running out of my room. When I was dressed and ready to go, we headed to the mall and I let my baby shop till she dropped. I guess Cherish told her she couldn't make it and that was cool with me, I wanted to spend some quality time with my baby anyways.

"Daddy, can I get the purple Timbs?"

"Yeah, go ahead," I said walking into Kids Foot Locker.

"Hey, Jason," I heard someone say.

"Oh what's up Kaliah, what you doing here?" I said hugging her.

"Shit, buying my nephew some sneakers."

"What's up lil nigga?" I said, dapping her nephew up.

"What's up?" he replied before running off to find him some sneakers.

"So when am I gonna repay you for making me feel better?"

"I don't know; I got a hot date tonight so that's a no go."

"Oh shit, aight then let me know when you're free."

"Daddy, mommy came!" Jas ran up to me screaming. Right behind her was Cherish giving me the evil eye and I could give zero fucks.

"Oh what's up lil mama, I didn't think you were coming."

"I bet you didn't, are you gonna introduce me to your friend?"

"My bad, lil mama this is Kaliah, Kaliah this is my baby mom."

"Baby mom?" Cherish questioned with her hands on her hips.

"It's nice to meet you," Kaliah said politely, sticking her hand out for Cherish to shake, only for her to play Kaliah out.

"Well call your daughter's phone when you're done, we're going to go blow your money," she said, grabbing Jas's hand and walking away.

"She seems pretty salty for someone who broke up with you," she said laughing.

"These pregnant chicks are crazy," I said shaking my head.

"Aight, well imma hit you up later and let you know how this date went," she said hugging me and walking away with her nephew. Calling Jas to see where they were, I met them in the food court for some lunch, and the whole time Cherish had an attitude.

"What's up with you?" I asked.

"So is she the reason for this new attitude?" she asked.

"No, you're the reason for it. I ain't gonna keep on chasing you when I know you don't want to be caught," I said honestly.

"Whatever, I'm taking Cherish with me to Camille's," she said before attempting to get up.

"Naw I want to spend some time with her so she's gonna stay with me for the rest of the day," I said, shutting her down.

"Oh ok." she said sadly before getting up to leave. I wanted to stop her, but I knew that's what she wanted me to do, so instead, I let her go.

Chapter Twenty-Six (Cherish)

"I swear this nigga got life fucked up if he thinks I care about what he's doing."

"Bitch, we in the movie theater and this seems to be all you can talk about so obviously you care," Camille said rolling her eyes.

"Whose side are you on?"

"I'm on your side, but if you love that man then stop with the games before he leaves your ass."

"Says the queen of games," I said sarcastically.

"Touché bitch, touché, but I had someone that loved me let me know when the games were getting out of control."

"So you think he's about to leave me for good?" I asked, scared.

"I don't know, but do you really want to take that chance?" she said before the previews started to come on. We were here to see *The Visit,* a movie I've been wanting to see for weeks. I wanted to say more, but the previews were my favorite part, so I kept quiet.

"Oh shit," Camille whispered.

"What's wrong?"

"Ummmm I see why you worried, baby girl bad as hell," she said looking across from us. Following her eyes, they landed smack dab on Mega and the bitch from the mall. I didn't think I would get as upset as I was, but that shit had my fucking blood boiling.

"No the fuck he didn't!"

"Girl, you better stop playing and get your man!"

"Hell naw, fuck him!"

"Looks like you're the one getting fucked with no Vaseline," Camille said with her brutally honest ass.

"She ain't that cute, is she?"

"Oh mama bad, but she ain't got shit on you."

"Really?"

"Really bitch. Do you wanna leave?" Camille asked.

"I ain't gonna let them run me out of the damn movies, Camille, fuck that."

"My bitch, well act like they ain't here and enjoy the movie," she said. The whole time the movie was playing, I couldn't even enjoy it because I was so busy watching them. I needed to see how they interacted so I could get a better feel of how into her he was. I watched as he put his hand across the top of her chair, and I saw how when the scary parts came on, she leaned over to his side. I didn't know what to think about this shit, but I knew I had to do something, sooner than later.

"I can't do this!" I snapped when the movie was almost over. Jumping up from my seat, I waddled my ass to their section, which took a lot longer since my big ass stomach was in the way.

"Really, Jason!" I snapped, standing in front of them.

"What you doing here?"

"No, what the fuck you doing here and why are you with her?" I said through teary eyes.

"Cherish, it ain't even like that damn, you making a scene and shit over nothing."

"Yo, sit ya big ass down!" I heard someone scream.

"Mind y'all fucking business!" I snapped, to say I was in rare form was an understatement.

"Yo, chill out, we'll talk about this later. Who you here with?"

"Fuck that, we gonna talk about this now!"

"Look, it isn't what you think," the girl he was with tried to explain.

"You definitely need to mind your fucking business, wit ya homewrecking ass!" I snapped.

"Wait, home wrecking, didn't you break up with him?"

"So you tell her our business, Jason?" I asked hurt.

"What the fuck, tame ya bitches nigga!" a ratchet girl with her friend said.

"Bitch, you the bitch!" Camille said. I didn't even know when she had come over to us, but I was glad she did. Before I knew what was happening, a big ass argument had popped off, but the crazy part about it is, Jason's little friend was on our side defending us, which was weird to me. I looked over at Jason and he had a look of disappointment in his eyes, which let me know that I was wrong as hell right now. Grabbing Camille's arm, I tried to force her to leave, but she wasn't budging at all and I wasn't gonna hurt myself or my babies in the process. It didn't take long for the police to come.

"Get ya fucking hands off me!" Camille screamed trying to get out of the officer's grip. Slamming her down on the theater floor, all hell broke loose.

"Don't you fucking slam her like she a man!" Jason said, rushing over to the officers. I couldn't help the tears that fell from my eyes as I stood handcuffed, watching them shove Camille's face into the ground.

"Don't fight back Cam, that's what they want!" I screamed.

"Fuck these police!" she screamed as they handcuffed her.

"You muthafuckas is gonna feel my wrath!" Mega's friend screamed.

"Oh shut the fuck up!" the cop snapped, mushing her. I watched as her eyes turned red and she didn't scream or curse, she just smiled.

"I want to know how this all started," the cop said. He got very upset when no one answered him, this was no longer about an argument, this was about how we were being treated. After laying on the ground for five minutes, Mega couldn't take it anymore.

"Yo, my girl pregnant with twins, she don't need to be laying on the fucking ground!"

"Yeah let her up!" a few bystanders screamed out.

"She gets up when I say so!" he said with a smirk. After about three more minutes, he helped me up and we were all taken to the county jail. All the females were together, not in a cell or anything like that; we were just cuffed and seated on benches.

"I'm sorry I got you into this Cam," I said as tears fell from my eyes.

"Don't be sorry, I would do it again!" she said seriously. Looking at her face, she had a rug burn on the side of her cheek, but overall she was ok and for that, I was thankful.

"I apologize to you too, and I appreciate you for helping me and my friend," I said to the girl.

"I tried to explain to you, me and Jason aren't like that, we actually met because of you and we are just friends," she said bursting my fucking bubble. I felt bout stupid as hell.

"Wow, I'm so sorry," I said.

"It's cool. I would've done the same thing for my man. I'm Kaliah by the way."

"Y'all shut up!" an officer snapped.

"Don't I have a right to a fucking phone call!" Camille snapped.

"Yeah, eventually," he said with a smirk.

"Imma get us out." Kaliah said with a smile.

"Excuse me officer, can I please have my phone call now?" she said nicely.

"Yeah, stand up," he said before uncuffing her and walking her over to his desk phone. She called someone and explained the entire situation from beginning to end before handing the police officer the phone.

"Well no sir... but I ... they were... Yes sir," he said hanging up with his mouth wide open.

"I'm sorry about this Ms. Williams," he said before walking over to us and uncuffing us.

"Oh wait, I want everyone that you arrested to be released right now, especially Jason Cruz."

"Yes ma'am," he said before picking up the phone and dialing a number.

"Well damn, who are you?"

"I'm nobody, but I went on a hot date the other night with the district attorney," she said before laughing.

"Damn, you must have left a lasting impression," Camille said, high fiving her. We waited outside for Mega to be released, and when he finally came out, he didn't even look my way.

"Mega, I'm sorry."

"Cherish shut up talking to me right now, aight," he said through gritted teeth.

"I didn't mean to act that way or for any of this to happen," I tried to explain.

"Cherish, you're fucking young as hell. You ended shit with me, which I understood, but then when I tried to make shit right, you weren't tryna hear shit I had to say. Then you see me with someone and act like a fucking spoiled child, you don't even know this woman or our relationship, but you didn't care!" he said shaking his head and walking away.

"I fucked up and now he doesn't love me anymore," I said crying.

"He loves you, trust me, I'll talk to him," Kaliah said before walking away.

"You fucked up, but he'll get over it," Camille said hugging me. When I finally got home after picking up my car, I was defeated and tired as hell. After showering, I laid in the bed calling Mega. I had called him over twenty times and he had yet to answer or call me back. Fuck this, I wasn't gonna let him shut me out. I had something to say to his ass and he was gonna hear me out tonight. Getting out of bed, I threw my slippers on and headed down the stairs to go to his house. While walking down the steps, I missed a few of them and went tumbling down the stairs. I only fell on my ass so I was almost certain that the babies were just fine, but when I tried to get up, my ankle hurt like hell, causing me to scream out. Grabbing my phone, I called Mega only to have him not answer my phone call. Giving up, I called Camille and she answered on the first ring.

"What's up boo?" she asked.

"I fell down the steps and I hurt my ankle, I keep trying to get up, but I can't."

"You're not supposed to attempt to get up when you fall while pregnant until you get checked out. Call 911 and let them know what's going on, I'm on my way," she said, frantic as hell.

"Can you call Jason?"

"Yeah, I got you," she said before hanging up.

Chapter Twenty-Seven (Mega)

"Man I don't give a fuck what you say; I ain't talking to her ass!"

"Come on now, how did you think she was gonna react seeing you with another woman? Plus her hormones are out of control," Kaliah said.

"Shit could have gone way worse than this."

"But it didn't," she said.

"Just answer her calls and find out what she wants to say to you."

"Naw I'm good, not right now," I said, ending yet another call from her. As we talked and drank, I still couldn't believe what the fuck went down earlier.

"I think you and Cherish are cute together. Shit, I would have done worse if you were my man," she said with a smile.

"I doubt you would have acted a fool like that over me," I said laughing.

"Naw you that nigga, you confident yet humble, you're loyal as hell, not to mention you fine as fuck," she said while rolling a blunt. I couldn't help but look at her sexy lips as she sealed the blunt to perfection. I don't know what I was thinking. Fuck it, I know what I was thinking. I needed some pussy and I wanted to get it from a chick I knew would appreciate it.

Standing up, I took the blunt from her lips. Grabbing her hand, I stood her up and looked over her sexy body. Twirling her around, I licked my lips as her ass shook lightly.

"Damn, you sexy as shit."

"I already know that," she said cockily before wrapping her arms around my neck and kissing me. It was so intense our tongues danced with each other hungrily. Taking a break from kissing, she undressed me slowly. I didn't have to make the first move, and I didn't have to question whether I was being too rough, I knew she wanted it. Pushing me onto the bed, she slowly undressed herself until she was wearing nothing. Straddling me, she licked my neck, down to my chest. Grabbing a condom from her nightstand, she unwrapped it before putting it into her mouth and slowly applying it inch by inch on my dick. All I could hear was tight suction as she devoured me into her mouth. Licking the tip of my dick, she swirled her tongue around before taking all of me into her mouth again. I don't know if the shit was really this good, or if I just hadn't had it in a long time, but she had a nigga gone off her sloppy toppy. I could feel her spit dripping down my dick onto my balls. I had to think about anything to keep myself from cuming. Damn did I eat today, did I turn all the lights off at the crib before I left. I was doing real good concentrating until I heard her gag and my seeds went all in her mouth and she swallowed that shit like it was the sweetest tasting treat she'd ever had. Switching to a new condom, she straddled my dick before slowly sitting on it.

She was wet as hell and gushy. With her hands on my chest, she rode me hard as hell. All that could be heard were the sounds of her pussy popping on my dick. Not wanting to let her get the best of me again, I flipped her over. Lifting her legs over my shoulders, I thrusted into her pussy roughly.

"Shit, Jason!" she screamed while clawing at my back. I continued to dig in her guts, long dick style. I felt her trying to scoot her ass back and dragged her right back where I wanted her.

"You wanted this dick, so take it," I said through gritted teeth. Turning her over, I had her face up, ass down. Slapping her ass, I dove in and hit her from the back with slow long strokes. Wrapping my hand around her neck, I tilted her head back and licked her neck lightly, causing her to shake. We fucked for over an hour before we were both worn out and satisfied. Grabbing the blunt from the nightstand, she lit it and we got high as hell. Looking at my ringing phone, I was surprised to see that it was now Camille calling me. I was about to press end because it was probably Cherish, but I decided to answer.

"Yo. what's up?"

"Cherish fell down the steps, she tried to call you, but of course you didn't answer."

"Where she at, I'm on my way!" I said jumping up and grabbing my pants

"You might as well meet her at the hospital," Camille said with an attitude

"Well are you gonna tell a nigga what hospital she live close to."

"She'll be at Virtua, by you," she said before hanging up.

"Is everything aight?" Kaliah said kissing my back.

"Naw, Cherish fell down the steps!"

"Oh shit, I'm so sorry," she said sincerely, while rubbing my back.

"Yo, about this shit here…"

"It is what it is, you ain't gotta say nothing," she said nonchalantly.

"Aight bet," I said, dropping the subject.

"You want me to drive or you good?"

"I'm good, I'll call you later," I said before rushing out. When I got to the hospital, I was nervous as hell waiting for her to get here. When the automatic doors opened and I watched as my lil mama laid on that stretcher, I felt a déjà vu moment that made me sick to my stomach.

"You ok?" I asked rushing to her side.

"Sir, we need you to step aside," an EMT said.

"I love you lil mama!" I screamed before the doors closed. Camille walked in shortly after and I expected her to roll her eyes at me, but instead, she rushed into my arms.

"You think the babies are ok?" she asked.

"Yeah, they fighters like they mama," I said with a smile. We were there for about an hour before we were allowed back to see her. She had some things hooked up to her stomach, which scared the shit out of me.

"What are these for?"

"They just make sure the babies are good."

"And are they good?"

"Yes, I sprained my ankle, but everything is good."

"So when can you go home?" I asked.

"I don't know."

"Hello, I'm Doctor Carter, and Ms. Daniels and the babies are fine, but they are a little stressed."

"Stressed from what?" I asked.

"We don't know, but if she is stressed, it puts stress on the babies."

"So what do you suggest?"

"I suggest rest and love," he said with a smile.

"Ok, thank you."

"Either you come home with me, or you go with Camille, but you are not staying in that apartment alone," I said seriously.

"Alright damn, if I gotta be somewhere other than home then I want to be with you and Jas," she said surprising me.

"Ok," was all I said. When she was finally released, I helped her into my car and we headed home. I wanted her to come home ever since she left, but not this way.

"Are you still mad at me?" she asked.

"Cherish, I'm not talking bout this shit with you, my main concern is for you and the baby's safety, point blank."

"You're only saying you don't want to talk about it so that I won't be stressed, you gotta believe me when I say I didn't mean for shit to go that way."

"If you're not gonna believe my answers, then don't ask me questions," I said before turning the radio up. When we got home, the first thing she did was lay in our bed, Giving her extra pillows and her favorite blanket, she looked at home. Yeah I knew she missed being home, only if her ass wasn't so stubborn we wouldn't be going through this shit.

"You hungry?" I asked.

"Yeah, I could eat."

"What you want?"

"Hmmm cookies and pickles, but I want the sliced ones," she said, causing me to laugh. Damn, I missed her weird ass.

"Alright."

"What's so funny?"

"Nothing," I said walking out. When I came back with what she wanted, I walked in only to find her ass knocked out cold. Covering her up with a blanket, I walked out my bedroom and into the guest room. I wanted this to be comfortable for her so that she didn't fuck around and leave again, so if it meant me sleeping in the guest room, then so be it. Checking my phone, I saw I had a few missed calls. I knew they just wanted to know how Cherish was doing, so I sent a group text. As soon as I got comfortable and ready for bed, my phone started ringing. I saw it was Camille so I said fuck it and answered.

"Yo."

"Hey Jason, I don't mean to bother you, but is it possible you could meet me at the hall tomorrow for the baby shower."

"Do you need more money?"

"No, you gave me more than enough to cover everything, but I need your opinion on a few things."

"Aight, I can meet you at twelve."

"Don't play with me Camille!" I heard Mark snap.

"Listen, I'm sorry about the shit that went down at the movies, I should've kept my composure better."

"Naw you good Cam, I already know you're crazy," I said laughing.

"Yeah, but at the end of the day, I know you love Cherish and I need to stay out of shit."

"I accept your apology, and I appreciate you being a real friend to lil mama."

"Aight well imma let you go, I just had to let you know," she said before hanging up. It must be snowing in fucking hell; I never thought Camille would ever apologize to anyone, let alone me. I could've pointed out that I heard Mark in the background, so more than likely her ass got handed to her and he made her call me but shit, an apology is an apology. Lying back in bed, I thought about today and how those fucking cops were disrespectful and before I knew it, I had dozed off. Looking at my phone, it was nine in the morning and Cherish was lying beside me, naked. I don't know why she was sending mix signals, but I wasn't for the bullshit. Looking at her body as she poked her butt out, she was begging me to slide in without saying a word. I hopped up to take a cold shower, when I got out; she was already downstairs making breakfast.

"Do you miss me Mega?" she asked while making my plate.

"What you mean?" I replied, playing stupid.

"Come on now, do you miss me?" she asked on the verge of tears.

"Don't push this on me, this was what you wanted and I love you enough to give it to you," I said before smashing my breakfast. When I was done, I rushed out to meet Camille. Simply saying that shit to myself was weird to me, but I needed lil mama's baby shower to be perfect. When I got to the hall, it was set up nice, so I wasn't sure what she needed my opinion about.

"What's up Jason?"

"Oh hey, so what you need?"

"I don't know what food to have."

"Who's cooking?" I asked nervously.

"Don't worry nigga, it's being catered," she said rolling her eyes, causing me to laugh.

"Naw, but she likes anything, her favorites are fried chicken, potato salad, and snow crabs."

"Oh okay, do you like how this is set up?"

"Yeah, it's nice," I said ready to leave.

"Are you still giving her a hard time?" she asked.

"Man I'm giving her what she wanted."

"You know that girl loves you Jason."

"I love her too, but the same way she taught me a lesson, I gotta teach her one," I said with a smirk.

"I hear you. Well bring her here around five this evening."

"Aight," I said before leaving. When I got home after running around for a few hours, Cherish was sitting around looking like she'd lost her best friend and I was starting to feel like shit. When she saw me, she jumped up and rushed over to me. Wrapping her arms around my waist, she reached up and tried to kiss me.

"What up lil mama?" I said, lightly pushing her away.

"Nothing. What, I can't kiss you?"

"Man, first I wake up with you in the fucking bed with me, now I come in and you tryna kiss me, I already told you I'm not playing these games with ya ass. You don't know what you want and you ain't gonna be playing with my fucking emotions!" I snapped.

"I'm not trying to play with your emotions, you been distant as hell lately, I'm just trying to figure out where we at."

"You spent months pushing me away, so why wouldn't I be distant? Shit, maybe I need time to figure shit out just like you did."

"What you mean figure shit out, you don't know if you want to be with me now?"

"Naw, maybe I don't. I love you, but I don't deserve this shit. You push me away then try and pull me back just to see if you can, fuck kinda nigga you think I am."

"You being cold as hell and for what!" she snapped.

"Same reason you was. Ya ass made a fool out of not only ya self at that movie theater, but me too. You showed ya age and ya ass. I'm not that nigga for you if you feel you gotta act like that after you ended shit with me!"

"Fuck you Mega, fuck you. Obviously you don't want me here so drop me off at Camille's house please!"

"She ain't home, but for damn sure I will when she gets there. You wanna leave then go head, as long as you ain't going to that fucking death trap apartment, I don't care!"

"Whatever!" she screamed before sitting down and pouting.

"Man, fix ya face lil girl. Go get dressed, I wanna take you somewhere."

"Really, you wanna take me somewhere but it's obvious you still mad at me," she said.

"Man either get dressed or don't, but I'm leaving here without without ya stubborn ass. Damn, why you always got turn something into an argument!"

"You lucky I'm bored out of my mind here or else I wouldn't be going not a muthafucking place with your ass, and as soon as Camille gets home, you better drop me the fuck off!" she said, rolling her eyes.

"Well get dressed then and come on," I said, watching her rush upstairs as fast as her eight month belly could go. I didn't want to be mean to her, but shit chicks were crazy as hell. I buy her flowers, tell her I love her and I get her ass to kiss. When I ain't checking for her, a little mean to her, she runs around trying to please me and doing what I said. Hell if I would've known that cutting her ass off would have forced her to do a complete 180, I would have done it a long time ago.

"I'm ready," she said after taking almost an hour to get ready, but I wasn't gonna complain one bit.

"Aight come on," I said nonchalantly.

"Fuck you and stop talking to me," she said. When we headed out, I knew she had no idea where we were going. She knew Camille was throwing her a baby shower, but she didn't know when. Pulling up to the hall, I helped her out the car.

"Where are we, is it someone's birthday?"

"Yeah, come on," I said grabbing her hand and walking into the hall where friends and family stood excitedly. Camille filled it up and did the damn thing since lil mama ain't got no family. When I saw Cherish crying, I assumed they were happy tears, she looked so overwhelmed and happy.

"Why you crying lil mama?" I asked, wiping her tears.

"Because I'm a pregnant hormonal female, but I ain't forget about what the fuck you said to me!" she said rolling her eyes.

"You keep on rolling them shits and they gonna stay that way," I whispered to her.

"Here, let me get a picture of the happy parents!" Camille said snapping a few pictures.

"I know you're mad at me but..."

"Don't worry mad or not this night is about my babies and I wouldn't mess that up for nothing," I said.

"Ooooo Mega this picture came out nice!" Cherish said holding Camille's phone. They had a photographer here, but Camille wanted all the pictures she could get.

"Let me see!" I said looking at the pictures and sending them to myself so I could post them on Facebook and the gram.

"So we gonna play some games!" Camille said hyped.

"Oh God, how do you play?" Cherish asked.

"Well I have five poopy pampers and whoever figures out what the poop is made of wins a prize."

"That is so nasty, but I wanna play," Cherish said laughing. I didn't know this baby shower game shit, hell this was my first baby shower, I always thought they were only for chicks. On top of that, I wasn't feeling lil mama at all, her ass was on punishment, and this baby shower ain't change that. I would be back when they needed me, but until then, I was going out to smoke with my niggas.

Chapter Twenty-Eight (Jayda)

Oh yeah, y'all thought I was gone, ran scared, paleeze it's gonna take more than some threats to stop me from getting my man, I just had to regroup. I wasn't expecting that little bitch Jasmine to say anything to Jason about what I'd said to her, and when she did, that put a serious wrench in my plans. Yeah it was me; I tried to run the bitch Cherish over. They wanna be at the doctor's like they the perfect family, naw bitch, ya man in love with me. If it wasn't for her being pregnant, he would be with me.

"Bitch, what you thinkin bout?" Ashley asked.

"I just want my man, and I don't want this bitch in the way," I said, taking back another shot. We were at a local bar getting wasted. Grabbing my phone, I did my hourly check of Jason's social media accounts and was taken aback when I saw a picture of him rubbing Cherish's stomach. I could have thrown up in my mouth, I was literally sick to my stomach.

"What's wrong?"

"Nothing. They posting pictures about this damn baby shower that should be my baby shower!" I said smashing my glass on the bar table.

"Yo, you can't do that here!" the bartender said.

"Chill out, she'll pay for it," Ashley said rolling her eyes.

"I can't believe while I'm here in pain, he's with her celebrating babies that she doesn't even deserve to have," I said as tears fell from my eyes. From the moment I met this bitch, she ain't been nothing but a pain in my ass, and I was tired of it.

"Well, why not just go get your man? Fuck that bitch, we both know it's you that he loves," she said hyping me up.

"I don't know, I just don't want him to think of me as ratchet."

"Girl, men like it when they wife get a little ratchet every now and again, you gotta claim what's yours."

"You're right!" I said getting up and clumsily walking to my car. After putting the address he had on Facebook into my GPS, me and Ashley drove to the baby shower. Pulling up, it was packed outside, but I knew this was what I needed to do for me. I couldn't leave this hall without my man, I refused to.

"You can do this Jayda."

"Bitch, I'm nervous."

"You look good. Ya makeup on fleek, outfit on fleek and you bad as hell, what you nervous for, that bitch should be nervous!"

"I do look good, don't I?" I said before checking my face and adding some MAC lip gloss to my lips."

"Imma stay out here, hurry up and go get ya man!" she said. When I got out the car, I strutted into the crowded hall.

Scanning the room for Jason, I walked boldly up to him while he sat next to Cherish, opening gifts.

"Can we talk?"

"Jayda, what the fuck you doing here!" he snapped.

"I came to get you; I'm tired of waiting for you to leave this bitch!" I said grilling Cherish while everyone stared at me with their mouths open.

"Oh, you a bold bitch!" Cherish said with a smirk.

"Always bold, never scared," I said rolling my eyes.

"I don't want you Jayda, never did. I don't want shit to do with you, and if you know what's best for you, ya ass will stay away from my girl!"

"Why you talking to me like this?" I asked Jason.

"Yo, you need to go!" Mark said, trying to grab my arm.

"Nigga, don't touch me!"' I said yanking my arm.

"Mega I love you, don't you understand that!" I said as tears fell from my eyes. I looked around and noticed Camille staring at me like she always did.

"Bitch, what you staring at!" I snapped at Camille.

"Oooooh shit, Jayden?" Camille screamed covering her mouth. I couldn't believe she actually figured out who I was.

What are the chances of Cherish befriending my fucking first cousin?

"What you mean Jayden, my name is Jayda," I said playing it off.

"Jayden, come on now, our mothers are sisters, you didn't think I would eventually recognize you!" Camille said shocked.

"You don't know what you're talking about, mind ya business, damn!" I snapped. This bitch was always in somebody business, even when were younger. Like bitch know ya role, shut the fuck up and play the background.

"You come to crash my friend's baby shower that I planned, you got me fucked up, this is my business. You running around getting sex changes that cost an arm and a leg while ya mama can barely keep her head above water. Yeah you should have had a sex change since you being such a fucking bitch!" Camille snapped.

"Wait, what the fuck is going on?" Cherish asked, confused.

"Girl I knew I knew her from somewhere, this bitch is a man!" Camille screamed to Cherish.

"Wait, so this whole time this nigga had me competing with a whole fucking nigga, this nigga fell for a fucking nigga, bitch!" Cherish screamed.

"Wait, Jayden who?" Mega asked, even more confused.

"She means Jayden, ya best fucking friend, nigga!" Cherish snapped.

"Don't listen to her," I said to Mega. I didn't need him believing this bitch. As I got closer in his space, he stared at me with confused eyes then began banging his forehead into the palm of his hand.

"I should've seen it; I can't believe I didn't see it!" Mega said pacing the floor back and forth with his head in his palm.

"Please don't be mad, I did what I needed to do for us," I pleaded with Mega.

"For who? Not us, there will never be a fucking us, you tried to kill my girl," Mega said through gritted teeth.

"I know that was a little off the wall, but I knew she was the only thing keeping you from loving me," I pleaded. He need to understand that I did this for us, not to trick him, but to simply show him that under different circumstances, we could be together and I could make him so happy. *The night I told Jason how I felt about him, it didn't go as I had planned. He ended up giving me an ass whooping out of this world and telling me he never wanted to see me again. I knew he had to save face because if he would of been honest about his feelings for me, Cherish would have told everyone and he would've lost all respect from the niggas in the hood. Limping out of his apartment, I hopped in my car and headed home. Deep in my thoughts, it finally hit me what I needed to do to win him over. Grabbing all the money that I had, I bought a plane ticket and took the first flight to Atlanta. Looking online, I found one of the best plastic surgeons in Atlanta and started my transformation. The doctor gave me my first of many hormone replacement therapy sessions. Shortly after completing the therapy sessions, I underwent my first surgery, which was a facial feminization surgery. Most trans women don't do this surgery, but I needed it to be as believable as possible. What's the point in paying all this money and going through all this pain just to end up a manly woman. Next were my ass and breasts, then my voice. They do have a surgery for it, but I opted against it and just went ahead and got speech lessons to feminize my voice, kinda like training it to sound a certain way. I even got a tracheal shave, which didn't cost as must as I thought it would. This was excruciating pain, but it got rid of the bulge in my neck that most people call an Adams apple. I was in pain for months after getting all this surgery, and many times wanted to quit, but I kept my eyes on the prize and looked at the bigger picture. In the end, I would have my man all to myself. By the time I was finished with all my surgeries, I was dead broke and living in a motel. When I finally healed, I was shocked at how sexy I was and I knew the perfect way to get the money I needed was to use what I had paid so much money for. I started working at a gentlemen's club, none of them bitches liked me because I was fine as hell and I knew it. The only bitch that didn't see me as competition was Ashley. She didn't have too much of a shape, but she could shake that ass like no other, and that made her a lot of money. We instantly clicked and started fucking niggas together for the big bucks. I don't understand why every bitch wasn't out here sucking and fucking, I was raking in over ten grand a night. Shit, if I would have known being a woman was this lucrative, I would have done it a long time ago. The only problem I had with Ashley's ass is that she had a serious addiction to sniffing coke. I didn't fuck with drugs so I told her if she wanted to roll with me, she had to get clean. I thought she got clean because she wanted to get this money, but I soon found out that she was in love with me. Stupid bitch. Hell, I loved to dive in some pussy every now and again, but if I wanted a girlfriend, I would have kept my dick. My sole goal was winning over Jason, so as soon as I saved up enough money to look the part and hold me over, I took my ass back to Jersey with Ashley on my coattail.*

"This some Jerry Springer type shit. Jason you don't see them grown man shoulders and that linebacker back," Mama Betty said shaking her head and snapping me out of my memories.

"Mega, I did all this for you. All this pain, I did this so you could be proud to have me on your arm!"

"You tried to trick me, tried to have me looking real funny in these fucking streets," Mega said in a low tone. Before I knew what was happening, Mega punched me dead in the fucking face and proceeded to pound me. As he continued to rain blow after blow to my face, all I could think about was the damage he was doing. I felt myself going in and out of consciousness and was happy as hell when I heard my best friend's voice.

"What the fuck, get him off of her. Y'all niggas just sitting around letting this nigga pound on a fucking female!" she snapped trying to pull him off me.

"Female, naw boo that's a nigga named Jayden!" Camille said with a smirk.

"Wait, what, a nigga?" Ashley said.

"Yes a nigga, like had a dick between his fucking legs when he was born kinda nigga!"Camille snapped.

"Mommy, you came back for me?" Jasmine said running up to Ashley. Hearing his daughter must have snapped him out of his angry rage because he stopped hitting me and looked up at Ashley.

"So you were a part of this shit the whole time!" Mega screamed.

"Mega?" Ashley said with a confused look.

"Don't play stupid bitch, you don't even tell me I got a fucking kid then you leave her at my doorstep and never fucking look back!"

"Fuck you, I tried to tell you I was pregnant but you didn't want shit to do with me!"

"You were fucking the whole group home, fuck you mean. Had I of known it was my child I would have stepped up!"

"Oh, like you stepped up with ya new little girlfriend. She gets a baby shower, the nice cars and I bet you wanna marry her, why couldn't I get that? Maybe if I felt like you would have married me I would have told you!"

"Girl this man just said you were fucking everybody and they daddy and you didn't even deny it. You were running around busting it open, but you want somebody to make you their wife. You little girls got the world fucked up, ain't no man gon want a woman that done fucked half the world with ya football field pussy!" Mama Betty said.

"Bitch mind ya business and eat ya food wit ya wide ass!" Ashley screamed at her.

"Oh, I got ya bitch!" Mama Betty said getting up. She had always been a firecracker and I always liked her, she treated us like family whenever we came around.

"Wait, mommy? Bitch you didn't tell me you had kids!" I snapped.

"You late as hell and you didn't tell me you used to be a nigga, so we even," Ashley said with an attitude.

"Where the fuck you been!" Mega said charging towards Ashley.

"I had to go take care of myself; I ain't no good to my baby in the state I was in," Ashley said.

"Man, I would have taken her regardless, but for you to just drop her off and run…"

"So you got ya fucking stalking ass thirsty bitch here, and now I find out you got ya baby mom here too crashing my fucking baby shower!" Cherish screamed.

"Babe, I didn't know any of this was gonna happen," Mega tried to explain.

"I ain't come to crash shit, hell I didn't know nothing about this, I'll just take my baby and be on my way."

"I don't wanna go with you, I wanna stay with Daddy and Cherish," she said running behind Mega's legs.

"You ain't taking my fucking daughter, if that's what you came for, you can leave now!" Mega snapped.

"Hell you come in here tryna take a girl that don't even wanna go with you, it's been almost a year and we ain't heard shit from you, and we liked it that way!" Cherish snapped.

"Bitch, you were playing mommy, but I'm the real one."

"Shit, I can't tell." Camille said while Jas hid behind Mega and Cherish.

"Man fuck her, fuck everybody, I love you!" I snapped. I hated that this was becoming less and less about me, and more about the other bullshit. I need Mega to see that I am the one that truly loves him.

"Imma kill this nigga!" Mega said reaching for his waist, before realizing Jasmine was staring at him.

"Get the fuck out!" Cherish screamed.

"Calm down Cherish, don't forget you're pregnant," Camille said walking Cherish over to some chairs. While she was walking, I noticed all the dudes beginning to circle me and Ashley, but not before Cherish screamed in pain.

"My water broke!" she screamed before everyone rushed to her. Using this as an opportunity to get the fuck out of dodge, I grabbed Ashley's arm and hauled ass. When we got into the car, Ashley wasted no time trying to question me, but I wasn't tryna hear that shit right now.

"So you in love with my baby dad?" she asked as if she didn't already know the answer.

"Yes, I didn't know he was your baby dad, you didn't even tell me you had any kids."

"I know they can't be telling the truth, did you really use to be a man?" I asked.

"Bitch, shut up with all the questions, damn!" I snapped. I hated to be called a man. Jayden left a long time ago when I confessed to Mega that I was in love with him back at his apartment. I thought for sure he felt the same way. Growing up in the hood, you're looked down on for being gay, they automatically think you're a bitch, so I understood why he reacted the way he did. I changed for him, for us, so that we could live normal lives together, but here this bitch Cherish go fucking it up once again.

"Are you mad at me?" Ashley asked.

"I know why I didn't tell you about my past, because I paid too much fucking money for my present, so fuck my past, but I don't understand why you wouldn't tell me that you had a whole fucking daughter. Shit, is there anything else I don't know?"

"No, you know everything Jayda. I didn't tell you because I was ashamed. When I had Jasmine, I was young, shit I'm only twenty-two and she's almost ten years old. My uncle was raping me every day, and when social services found out from my neighbor, they took me away and sent me to a group home, that's how I met Jason. He was in love with me, but all I wanted was to fuck as many men as I could. I felt wanted and loved, as crazy as that may seem. One day he caught me fucking the group home manager in the closet; he was heartbroken and wanted nothing to do with me. Shortly after, he left the group home and a few days after, I found out I was pregnant. I could have found him, but I honestly didn't think he was the father. I blamed it on the group home manager, he was older, so I assumed he had money, but I was wrong. He moved me into his roach infested apartment that he shared with his cousin. I wasn't even mad, shit, what he gave me was more than my own mama ever gave me. He was really nice to me until I had Jasmine, she didn't look anything like him and shit went downhill from there. He had me tricking and introduced me to coke. I never wanted to have Jasmine, but didn't have money for an abortion, and nobody believed they were the dad except that nigga and he told me I wasn't killing his baby. I started leaving her at home by herself, not feeding her, shit, I was a child myself, I wanted to have fun and do shit. The only thing important to me was tricking, partying and getting high. One morning after a night of partying, I came home to find him molesting my baby. I may have been a junky, and maybe I never did right by her, but I refused to let her go through the same shit I went through, so I found his address and dropped her off. I didn't get out the car, didn't even write a letter, I told her the apartment number and pulled off. After a few days of tricking, one of my girls told me she was moving to Atl, said that was where the money was. I didn't have shit for me here, so I went with her.

"Damn, you just dropped ya baby off with the nigga, you really ain't shit," I said with a smirk.

"So after everything I just told you, that's all you took from it?"

"Yup," I said shrugging. I didn't give a shit and I didn't have time to be throwing no pity party for the next bitch.

"I'm tired of you treating me like shit!"

"I treat you how you treat ya self bitch, so miss me with that shit!"

"Whatever, so what's the plan?" she asked.

"I don't even know if I can trust you anymore."

"For real, after everything we done been through you want to question my loyalty!"

"Bitch get out your feelings, I don't trust nobody. But after finding out who you are, I definitely don't trust you!"

"I can't believe you would say that to me."

"So you really expect me to believe that I just ran into your ass at the club, of all the states, of all the clubs," I said shaking my head.

"I am fucking loyal to you, I love you. Do you know how hard it's been to see the person I love fight so hard to get the next."

"If you really love me, prove it!"

"Just tell me what you need me to do."

Chapter Twenty-Nine (Cherish)

"Don't fucking say shit to me!" I said putting my hand up for Mega to shut the fuck up.

"Jason, please go sit over there, she doesn't want you near her," Mama Betty said shaking her head.

"Come on so we can get you into the car."

"Imma follow y'all!" I heard Mega scream.

"Nigga you best stay where the fuck you at, I don't wanna see your fucking face!" I said holding my stomach in pain while bending over when another contraction came.

"Are you sure you don't want him there?" Camille asked.

"I'm positive, this nigga might fuck around and have them bitches in the delivery room fighting, I ain't got time for the drama that comes with Mega, not right now!" I snapped.

"I swear of all the baby showers I done been too, I ain't never seen no shit like this. You got trannies, baby mama's fighting, this better than a book," Mama Betty said shaking her head.

"Please, just help me get her into the car," Camille said rolling her eyes.

"Chile you go head and roll them eyes at me again imma knock them bitches out!" Mama Betty snapped, causing me to burst out laughing.

"I can't believe this shit; I can't catch a break at all," I said as Camille drove me to the hospital.

"Yeah, that was some bullshit."

"So how do you know Jayden?"

"That's my cousin."

"What?"

"Yeah, girl. We were tight as hell when I was younger, but something happened and my aunt sent him with his dad. I saw him a couple times when we were in high school, but not much. He got my auntie eyes, which is how I finally figured out who he was."

"I can't get over this shit, the drama is like never ending and I'm so tired of it," I said as she pulled up to the hospital.

"Come on boo," Camille said helping me out of the car and into the hospital.

"Thank you," I said sincerely.

"You know I got you. Can somebody please help my friend, her water broke!" she screamed loud as hell. Before I knew it, a nurse was sitting me in a wheelchair and pushing me into labor and delivery. Laying me on the bed, a nurse came in and gave me an ultrasound. I felt so disgusting as the amniotic fluid continued to pour out of me.

"I'm going to see how many centimeters dilated you are, it may feel a bit uncomfortable, but it shouldn't hurt."

"Is all this fluid normal?" I asked the nurse.

"Yes, it's normal, some women have more than others," she said before sticking her fingers in me, causing me to jump a little.

"Wow, you are six centimeters dilated, ninety percent effaced," she said.

"What does that mean?"

"Means you almost about to deliver girl," Camille said hyped.

"Yeah, and the contractions should get much stronger," the nurse said.

"Stronger then this?"

"Yes, did you want an epidural?"

"No, I have my care plan in my purse," I said motioning for Camille to hand me my purse. After two hours of contractions, I was in excruciating pain.

"You ok boo?"

"No bitch I ain't ok, I changed my mind, I can't do this!"

"It's too late to be changing your mind, they coming with or without you."

"Well I want Mega; I need him, gimmie my phone!" I snapped.

"Calm down, Cherish," she said handing me my phone. Dialing Mega's number, I listened as it rang and prayed that he answered. While waiting for him to answer, another contraction hit me so hard I screamed out in pain.

"Lil mama!" I heard Mega scream worried.

"I hate you so much right now, but I need you, please come!" I said crying.

"I'll be up there in a minute," he said hanging up on me. As soon as he walked in and saw me, he rushed to my side. I could tell he was still a little stand offish, but I didn't care as long as he was here.

"Your care plan states that you wanted water births."

"No I don't want to do that anymore," I said as Mega squeezed my hand gently. I couldn't explain my feelings, it's like as mad as I was at him for being the cause of all this drama on a day that was supposed to be for us to celebrate our babies, I couldn't imagine going through this with anyone but him. Not Camille, not Mama Betty not anyone but him. He gave me strength when I felt like I had none, confidence and security. Just being around him made me feel like I could do anything.

"How you feel?"

"I feel fine; I'm just ready to see my babies," I said smiling. I went from feeling relaxed to feeling nothing but pain.

"I feel like I have to shit."

"Oh shit, that means the babies are coming!" Camille said smiling.

"Go get the nurse!"

"Mega, I swear I hate you for doing this to me!" I screamed while squeezing his hand.

"Come on, it's almost over," he said rubbing my back.

"I don't hate you I love you, I'm sorry. Oh my God, it hurts, Mega help me," I screamed before placing my legs in the stirrups myself and giving into the urge to push.

"Cherish are you pushing? I don't think you supposed to be pushing without the doctor!" he said with a scared voice.

"I can't fucking help it, my body is telling me to push, so that's what I'm doing. You better get to the bottom of this fucking bed and catch my babies!" I snapped at him.

"You ok? What the fuck, somebody get the nurse damn, it's blood on the bed," Mega screamed. I didn't know what was happening, I felt Mega holding my hand while wiping my sweat with a cold rag, while I continued to push. By the time the doctors and Camille came in, Mega had my baby girl in his arms and for a moment, the pain went away.

"Oh my God, Cherish, she's beautiful!" Camille cooed. After Mega cut the cord and the nurses took the baby to clean her off, they gave her to me and I couldn't help but kiss her beautiful face. She had my chocolate skin and Mega's beautiful almond shaped eyes. Enjoying my baby girl didn't last long because shortly after, another burst of pain hit me hard.

"Fuckkkkk please take her, oh my God it hurts!" I screamed. I pushed twice and out came my baby boy at 5 lbs 6 oz. He looked like I played no parts in making him, he was Jason's twin. He was so handsome; both of my babies were beautiful. I was so tired I could feel myself drifting off to sleep; having these babies took a toll on me.

"Why she look like that?" I heard Mega ask.

"She's hemorrhaging, I need you two to leave the room!" the doctor screamed.

"No I ain't leavin shit!" Camille snapped.

"I promise I will do my best, but you guys really need to leave so I can work," he said. I couldn't feel and hear Mega anymore after that. When I woke up, I was in a different room and I didn't see my babies, I instantly began to panic. Were they ok, did something happen? Hitting my call button over and over, I waited for someone to come into my room.

"Oh you're up, how are you feeling?"

"I'm feeling ok, but where are my babies?"

"They're fine; you were sleep so we took them to the nursery."

"Where is Jason?" I asked.

"He's in the nursery with them, along with your sister," she said. Before I could ask any more questions, Jason and Camille walked into my room all smiles.

"I will be back, I'm going to go bring the babies down," the nurse said before leaving.

"They are beautiful Cherish!" Camille said.

"Yeah, they look like they daddy!" Mega boasted. The whole time we were in the hospital, he hadn't said much of anything to me if it didn't concern the babies, and that scared me. Maybe I took shit too far; maybe I shouldn't have ended things. I don't know what I should've done, but I knew I loved him and I couldn't handle not being with him or him not loving me anymore. As he sat in the chair feeding Jaleesa, I fed Jason Jr. and for a moment, our eyes connected and I thought I saw a glimpse of love, but it didn't last long before his attention was back on our beautiful Jaleesa.

Chapter Thirty (Mega)

Things with me and Cherish haven't been going good. I see my kids everyday and I hired a nanny so she could get a break. I asked her if she wanted to come back home so it would be easier to co-parent, and she turned me down. She's been home for over a month and the babies are doing really good. Sometimes I want to just say fuck the games and just tell her ass to come home so we can work things out, but she needs to grow and mature more before I can do that. She got so mad at me for them ruining her baby shower, but in all honesty, I can't control them bitches and she should know I would never intentionally hurt her. I been fucking with Kaliah, it ain't nothing serious, she cool as shit and we just friends who occasionally get high and fuck the shit out of each other. She ain't on that crazy stalker shit at all and promised that she knew what it was.

"What's up, how's fatherhood treating you?" Mark asked, walking into my crib. He stopped by to cop some weed. Yeah I had money, but the hustler in me wouldn't let that old habit die.

"Shit is great, I love all my babies," I said with a smile.

"How you and Cherish?"

"We don't really talk much, but we been co-parenting. Imma talk to her tonight and see if we can get some kind of understanding."

"Yeah you gotta be cool with ya kids' mom, that shit makes life a lot easier."

"You right about that. I see them every day and she has never tried to stop me from seeing them, but when I'm around, it's a lot of tension and I don't like that shit."

"What's up with you and that Kaliah chick? Y'all been spending a lot of time together."

"Man, she cool as shit and she knows what she wants."

"So, you feeling ole girl?"

"Like I said she cool, but I don't like her on that level."

"Come on now, you fucking that girl."

"A few times, but not really," I said laughing. Giving him his weed, we talked a little while longer.

"Be careful, shit can get real crazy real fast with these females," he said before getting up to leave.

"Naw, Kaliah cool, trust me," I said before closing the door. Sitting down, I guess we spoke her up because she was now calling my phone.

"What's up K?"

"Shit, I was about to go to Cherish's house and see the twins," she said.

"What made you do that?"

"She called and invited me; I couldn't be rude and be like naw."

"Oh aight, I'm bout to head over there too," I said before hanging up. I didn't like this shit, wasn't no reason in the world for them to be hanging out, but what could I say. I trusted Kaliah enough to believe that she wouldn't do shit to jeopardize my relationship with Cherish. Together or not, if she found out I was dealing with Kaliah in any way, all hell would break loose. Hopping in my car, I headed over to Cherish's house. When I parked, I was met by Kaliah who was walking up to Cherish's door.

"You coming over tonight?" she asked.

"I don't know, I got Jas."

"You can bring her," she said.

"I'll let you know," I said before knocking on Cherish's door. When she opened it, the first thing she did was hug Kaliah.

"Hey Jason, the kids are in their bouncers," she said nonchalantly. Walking into the kids' room, I scooped Jason Jr. first, then Jaleesa, out of their bouncers and took them into the living room.

"So what's been up? I'd been meaning to call you after I got out the hospital, but the twins keep me busy," Cherish said talking to Kaliah.

"Oh, girl it's cool, did you get the gifts I sent?"

"Yeah, I love the little Polo outfit you got for them, they wore it yesterday," she said before pulling out her phone and showing Kaliah pictures.

"They are so cute," Kaliah gushed.

"You want to hold Jaleesa?" Cherish asked.

"Oh no, I might get the baby bug," Kaliah said laughing.

"Girl please," Cherish said with a laugh before taking Jaleesa from me and handing her to Kaliah. As she held the baby, she looked a little nervous like she knew she had no business holding the daughter of the woman whose kids' father she was fucking, but Cherish was persistent as hell.

"She looks so much like both of you!" Kaliah gushed.

"So I was thinking about having a dinner, one I could invite everyone to to officially see the babies," she said with a smile.

"You don't think they're still too young to have all these people all over them, picking them up, touching all on their faces."

"It's only close friends Jason, ain't like I got many people I can show them off too," she said, rolling her eyes.

"Can you come in the room with me so we can talk?" I said before placing Jason Jr. into his swing."

"Yeah I guess, Kaliah can you watch them?" she replied before following me into the room.

"So how's therapy going?"

"It's going good, things are really good. I signed up for school the other day, I know I said no nannies, but thank you for hiring her."

"Wow, that's good lil mama, and no problem, I just want for you to be able to do most of the things you want, you know still have a life."

hat did you want to talk about?"

"I wanted to talk about us, we ain't together right now, but I miss our friendship. I don't want to argue or have things awkward with us."

"I agree, maybe we can start hanging out and focus on being friends while co-parenting."

"I would like that, so are you free tomorrow night?" I asked.

"Damn, I didn't think you would ask so soon," she said with an awkward laugh.

"The sooner the better."

"Aight, I'll call the nanny, does tomorrow at eight work for you?"

"That's cool," I said before hugging her. It wasn't one of those I love you hugs, just a friendly one, and I was cool with that. When we walked back into the living room, Kaliah had put Jaleesa to sleep. We all talked for a little bit before I felt like I was ready to go.

"Well imma head out," I said.

"I'm right behind you," Kaliah said. When we got outside, she voiced how uncomfortable she felt holding my baby.

"Man, this shit fucking with me. You know I think you cool, but maybe we should fall back."

"I understand, but me and Cherish ain't together."

"But she doesn't know about us and it doesn't feel right," she said, shaking her head and walking away. When I got home, I thought about everything that Kaliah said, and she was right. The last thing I wanted to do was hurt either of them, so maybe I needed to take a break from her until I figured this shit out between me and Cherish. The next day, I was both nervous and excited, tonight was the night that I took Cherish out on a date so we could discuss what was going on with us. After getting showered and dressed, I was ready to go pick up lil mama. When I got to her house, the nanny had already put the kids down for their nap. Walking quietly into their room, I kissed both of them before heading back into the living room. When Cherish walked out, I would be lying if I said those babies didn't make her badder than she already was, she looked more mature, and her body was bad as hell. Her breasts were bigger, and her ass was looking real right.

"Are we gonna leave, or are you just gonna stare at me?" she asked with a smirk.

"We leaving smart ass, come on," I said. When we got to the restaurant, it felt a little weird because we haven't done anything like this in a while.

"So what's been going on with you?" she asked.

"Shit, between the kids and the label, I'm busy as hell," I said.

"So you're not dating anyone?" she asked.

"I've been seeing someone."

"Wow, ok well congrats," she said not really meaning it.

"What about you?"

"I got the nanny, but a man is the last thing on my mind, I'm tryna live life."

"I feel you, so do you think we can be cordial?"

"We have been cordial Jason, naw we don't hang out, but at least we don't argue when we do see each other."

"I guess, but I want us to be friends"

"So you don't see us ever getting back together?"

"Lil mama you got some growing up to do, I can't answer that question."

"I was grown enough for you to fuck with, grown enough to have your babies, I was grown enough to do all those things, but now I'm not. I don't understand that, but I can't be mad at how you feel so ok," she said rolling her eyes. We ate and talked for the remainder of the night before I dropped her off back home.

Chapter Thirty-One (Cherish)

Dinner with Jason didn't really go as I had planned, but I was glad I did it, it showed me that I really needed to move on. Don't get me wrong, I didn't want to; I loved him with every part of me. I saw him as my hero, my saving grace, my everything, but I refused to sit around while he lived life and stayed stuck on him. Maybe I did have some growing to do, but shit I was seventeen fucking years old and he knew that before we got together. Today was the day of my get together, nothing extravagant, I just invited, Camille, Shana, Queesha, Kaliah, Chris, Kasan, Terrence and Mark. I called Mama Betty and tried to invite her, but she laughed in my ear and said bring her baby to see her tomorrow. That woman was a trip, but I loved her to the end. As I stood in the kitchen cooking, I heard the front door open. It had to be none other than Camille since she was the only one with a key.

"Hey boo," she said when she walked into the kitchen.

"Hey, thanks for coming."

"What you need me to do?" she asked.

"You can set the table."

"Girl, I can help you cook."

"No, I got it."

"Aight then," she said before walking out. I wish I would have her cook at something I was having and be the talk of the crew, naw I was good. When I was done cooking and everything was set up, people started coming. The first people to come were of course Camille and Mark since Camille had come to help. When everyone came they went straight for the babies, Queesha even cried. I felt so bad for her. I heard that she really wanted to give Chris children, but with her being HIV positive, it made it scary.

"They are adorable Cherish!" she gushed.

"Thank you, they are a handful though," I said laughing. As they bounced the babies around, Jason's ass stood watching while passing out hand sanitizer, I thought it was the cutest thing ever. When we all sat down to eat, we laughed and talked about everything under the sun from relationships, to parenthood, to politics and weed. We had a good time and it felt good to do something other than change shitty diapers and burp babies.

"We going out to smoke," Jason said before heading out with the boys, with Kaliah following them.

"Who is that bitch and why she going with them," Shana said.

"I introduced you already, that's Kaliah, and she went because she smokes," I said laughing.

"I don't trust bitches around my man," Queesha said rolling her eyes.

"Girl, don't nobody want Chris crazy ass but you!" Camille said, causing us all to laugh.

"Fuck all y'all!" she said while laughing.

"Naw but foreal, she cool as shit."

"Well, do you know Mega and her came together?" Queesha said.

"They friends Queesha, hell I met her through him."

"I'm just saying; you can't trust these bitches."

"I don't trust her, I trust Mega, he wouldn't do no shit like that. Plus he already told me he's dating someone, but I know it ain't her."

"Oh shit, he told you he was dating?" Camille asked.

did and I was a little upset, but not as upset as I thought I would have been. Now that I know he's seeing someone, imma have me some fun," I said seriously.

"I know that's the fuck right!" Shana said.

"I'm gonna be eighteen in a couple months, I'm tryna go out of state and turn up."

"Hell yeah!" Camille said laughing. When the men came back, we ended our conversation and everyone started getting ready to head out.

"Thank you all for coming, I had so much fun," I said happily.

"Yeah we need to do this more often," Queesha said hugging me. After hugging all the women, they left and I was by myself again. Going into the kitchen, I started cleaning up. I had my music on and I was in my cleaning zone while the babies slept. When I was just about done, I heard a knock on the door. Opening the door, no one was there but an envelope was hanging out of my mailbox. Grabbing it, I walked inside and sat on my couch. Ripping the envelope open, I found a DVD of some sort with the words watch me on it. I stuck it into my DVD player and pressed play, as I watched it, tears fell from my eyes. I never felt so betrayed and played in my whole fucking life, I wanted to turn it off, but my body wouldn't move and my eyes refused to leave the screen. I felt like my heart had literally been ripped out of my chest. I would expect something like this from anybody, but not him. Calling Camille, I waited for her to answer.

"Hey boo," Camille answered. I tried to reply, but I couldn't stop crying.

"Cherish, what's wrong?"

"Somebody just sent me a DVD of Kaliah and Mega fucking," I said through tears.

"Wait, what?" she said in shock.

"I'm going over there and if she's there, I'm killing the bitch!"

"Cherish no, she ain't worth it!" she screamed before I hung up. Grabbing the twins, I packed them into the car, making sure to put the DVD into my purse. I was gonna get answers whether he liked or not. Pulling up to Jason's house, I jumped out of the car with both car seats in hand. Ringing the doorbell and banging on the door, I waited for him to open it.

"What you doing here this late?" he asked nervously.

"Are you gonna let me and your kids in?" I asked.

"Yeah my bad, come in," he said grabbing the car seats and walking into the living room.

"So I just got the craziest thing put in my mailbox," I said with a smile.

"What did you get?"

"Imma show you, are you here alone?"

"Uh yeah, why you ask me that?"

"Just curious," I said getting up and walking around the house.

"What you doing Cherish, fuck is going on with you?"

"Do you know how much I love you Mega?"

"Yeah and I love you too, tell me what's wrong."

"I was ok with us not being together, shit, I was planning trips and everything and you know who I wanted to invite?"

"Who?" he asked.

"Kaliah. You know I thought she was cool as hell, maybe even a friend," I said before walking into the bedroom we used to share. Pulling the DVD out of my purse, I put it into the DVD player in the bedroom, but didn't press play.

"What's that?"

"Where is she Jason?"

"Where is who?"

"Kaliah, where is she?" I asked calmly.

"She must be at her house, it's late, why would she be here?" he lied.

"You know, you may think this is about you, and me not knowing how to move on, but this is about betrayal. Another bitch I almost considered a friend who gave me their ass to kiss, another bitch that said fuck me, I had that bitch around my fucking kids, she held my children all while fucking their dad!" I said, pulling out a gun.

"Cherish, this ain't even you right now, put that shit away!"

"That bitch need to come out of wherever she hiding at Mega!"

"Aight, you right, we been fucking around. I didn't wanna hurt you, I didn't know y'all would even become friends," he explained.

"This ain't about you; this is about her smiling in my fucking face while fucking you behind my back!"

"But we ain't together, you left me, this is what I mean by you need to grow the fuck up!"

"Fuck you, grow up my ass, where she at?" I screamed. I had no clue how to really use a gun, but my blood was boiling. I felt so hurt that I could care less right now.

"I'm right here," she said, walking out of the closet.

"So you came in my house, came to family functions, held my babies, and you didn't think I would want to know that you were fucking their dad. I had to find out like this!" I said pressing play on the DVD player. They watched shocked, hands over mouth as the video showed them fucking wild and crazy in numerous positions in the bed we use to share, the bed we bought together, the bed his fucking daughter has slept in. Pointing the gun at Kaliah, I tuned out her cries and apologies; I couldn't give two shits about what she had to say. As I stood there, I heard Camille's voice. I turned around and she was standing behind me.

"Don't do this shit Cherish, if this nigga got you like this, you don't need to be with him anyways."

"It ain't about him, it's about her, Tyree, Meeka and everybody else that said fuck me, everybody I considered a friend that said fuck Cherish!"

"You got ya babies downstairs while you up here doing this," Camille said shaking her head. Training my gun on Kaliah, my hand began to shake. It was like déjà vu. Maybe the dream I had about Meeka was really warning me about this shit. I refused to be the Cherish everyone hurt, the Cherish people walked all over. Cocking the gun, I knew what I needed to do.

To Be Continued..............

056970032

CPSIA information can be obtained
at www.ICGtesting.com
Printed in the USA
LVHW091725291218
602155LV00001B/12/P